I0658019

Senseless

Sensibilities

S.W. Campbell

Published by Shawn Campbell

Senseless Sensibilities

ISBN: 979-8-9870287-2-8

To Azilynn, may your days be happy and your years full of contentment.

Senseless Sensibilities

Table of Contents

Preface

Contained within these pages are thirty-six short stories written between October of 2013 and February of 2015. Reading back over them in putting together this collection, it seems strange to think of them as having been written nearly a decade ago, but here we are, so much further down the road and somehow not feeling so different than I did then. Perhaps that is just the way of the world.

I have chosen to call this short story collection *Senseless Sensibilities*, partly because I'm a person who enjoys a good alliteration, but also because I think it is an apt description of a good chunk of the stories I've written over the years. I've had multiple people describe my writing to me as slice of life, which is fair, given I do have a deep interest in finding the poignancy of the mundane, though at times I wonder if it's just a polite way of telling me my stories are sad. Reading back over what I've written, it's hard to deny that my stories are sad, with even the ones meant to be more comedy than drama containing at least sad undertones, which brings up all sorts of questions about my own default settings not just with writing, but also with life.

That being said, a default of sadness in my writing makes a lot of sense to me. After all, my writing began as an exercise in mental health improvement, purging the bad on paper so the good could more fully be enjoyed in real life, and though by the summer of 2013 my writing was shifting increasingly from autobiographical to fabrication, the reasons for its creation did not necessarily change. Ultimately, there are no lives which contain only the good, and if my stories tend to be sad, I do not see it as proof of a sad life, but rather just the manifestation of timing. When I'm happy I tend to prefer the company of others and when I'm depressed I tend to prefer my own company, the latter of which is more likely to result in solitary practices such as creative writing. Hence the underlying vein. Though to be fair, the blame could also probably be fully put on the essential fact that happy characters, and therefore happy stories, are pretty damn boring both to write and read.

Anyways, I guess that is a fairly roundabout way of not really explaining the title at all. In the end, if there's one thing I'm sure of, it's that no matter what situation we find ourselves in, we have to find some way for it to make sense, even if the way it makes sense to us doesn't make any sense at all. We all live in a chaotic randomness which we lovingly call existence, and we are all doing are level best to get by in whatever way we can. Trying to understand the senseless sensibilities of others is one of the great challenges of life, one which is only made more complicated by many people forgetting that understanding is not the same thing as condoning or agreeing. However, it is a challenge we must take on, for only in understanding the senseless sensibilities of others, do we have any hope in understanding the true senseless state of our own. See, not a bad title, at all. I've always thought I was pretty good at titles.

The year 2014, at least as of this writing, stands as the busiest year of writing in my life. On top of writing some 32 short stories, totaling over 208,000 words, I also completed the first draft of my first novel, *The Uncanny Valley*, and made over 500 short story submissions for publication, of which only 75 received more than a boilerplate rejection, good or bad, and only 4 were actually published. Despite the rather poor statistical showing, 2014 was when I first started feeling like a real writer. Though not one of the literary reviews which published my work had more than a few thousand readers, it didn't matter. Someone besides myself was finding value in my work, enough value to share it with a wider audience, and it made all the difference in the world. I was hooked, and what had started as a nice way to pass the time became an endeavor taking up an ever greater amount of time and effort.

Looking back, I think the decision to try and get my stories published was likely the spark which shifted my writing from mental health maintenance and navel gazing towards an exploration of the world around me. Trying to get stories published forced me to think not just about what I felt I needed to say, but also how I said it. Directness gave way to metaphor and bluntness to clever twists of phrase. If you want to get something published you have to think about your audience, and if you're thinking about your audience you have to think beyond yourself, which not only leads to being a more well-rounded writer, but also a more well-rounded person in general.

Anyways, I'm most definitely rambling now, which I'm guessing is not what you are here for. Reading back over these stories in making this collection, I found myself enjoying them just as much as when I wrote them, and I hope in reading them, you enjoy them as well.

As always, before I close, I will leave you with the reminder that as with any writing, those of you who know me or have known me might find pieces of yourself in these stories. If you do, or think you do, remember, fictional characters are often amalgamations of many people, and even when they're not, short stories are but windows into a moment, unable to capture the full breadth of who any of us truly are. There is no such thing as a complete story. Happy reading.

An Apple A Day

It was the crack of dawn. While his wife snoozed in their bed, Hank Edwards quietly put on an old t-shirt, faded jeans, and wool socks. He picked up his book from the nightstand, took one last look at Marie, her mouth hanging slightly open, and slipped downstairs to brew a pot of coffee. The smell of roasted beans permeated the kitchen. Hank stared out the window and watched the sun rise above the distant hills. Four months of sun rises. All slightly different, but individually indistinguishable in memory. Hank eyed the growing beams of light. He noted the position of the wisps of cloud. The shift of every shadow. He stared at the rising orb until dark spots flashed across his vision. The coffee went into a thermos. Hank put on an old pair of leather boots and slipped on his old Carhartt coat, noting the added weight in one of the pockets, and with the thermos and book in hand, went out the backdoor into the cool crisp air of fall.

The ground was tinged with a thin layer of melting frost. Hank inhaled deeply, smelling the air, scented with the rot and decay of what was once green and vibrant. It was a strong smell. A good smell. The world was quiet. Every step across the fallen golden leaves went off like a string of firecrackers. The closing of the door. The rustling of Hank's clothing. The sharp note of a songbird. All was unnaturally resonant. Hank knew he had to enjoy the peace now while it lasted. Soon the hills would echo with the sharp blasts of rifle fire. The first day of deer season had come.

The cellar door was held closed by an old screwdriver in the hasp. The screwdriver's wooden handle was gray with age. The darkness of the cellar was pushed away with the pull of a string. A single light bulb illuminated wooden boxes sitting on rough wooden shelves set against dirt walls. Apples, pears, potatoes, carrots, onions, and beets. It had been a good growing year in Marie's garden, and the boxes had all been refilled. Hank picked up an old metal pail and filled it with apples from one of the boxes. They were medium sized and green, tart to the taste, and likely to lead to regrets if too many were eaten. Bucket in hand, Hank turned off the light, and returned to the world above, securing the cellar door with the screwdriver.

Carrying the thermos, book, and bucket, Hank tromped down a well-trodden path from the house through packed wooden sentinels of elm and oak. Dappled sunlight broke its way through the tangle of gnarled branches and the dying leaves which still held stubbornly on. The declining angle of the trail made Hank's worn out knees scream in protest. Once Hank had been a carpenter, until the sale of his father's farm had made working unnecessary. What had been farmland was now a strip mall and houses. The sale had come in time to save Hank's back, but not soon enough to save his knees.

The first sounds of distant shots. The rapid series of a semi-automatic which made Hank snort derisively at the lack of skill exhibited. When his knees had still worked, deer season had been a big part of his year. The getting up before daylight. The sitting in the stand high above the ground. The waiting. The tension. The release. He had always used a bolt action. The slower reload time forcing a greater amount of patience and skill. His rifle, in its cabinet next to the washing machine, was covered with dust.

A quarter mile from the house the path ended next to a fence of green metal posts and bright new barbwire. Signs declaring government property and no trespassing were hung every hundred yards in both directions. A decaying lawn chair sat beneath an ancient oak. A deer call hung by a string from a nail hammered into the tree. Hank took the deer call and gave it a couple loud blasts. He sat down in the lawn chair, pulled out his pocketknife, and started cutting the apples into quarters, throwing them just on the other side of the fence. It did not take long. They came out of the trees showing no signs of fear. The does with their fawns trailing after. The bucks, with their antlers proudly held high, alone.

When he had started four months ago they had been cautious. They would approach slowly, stopping to wait and listen. Drawn by the apples, but spooked by the figure in the chair. They were braver than they should be. They did not understand the meaning of the words wildlife preserve, but they knew that the land along the creek was safe. Hank never made any sudden moves or noises. The first month he had just sat quietly in his chair, reading and drinking coffee, letting the repetition meld him into the surrounding scenery. The second month he had started getting up and walking around. Spooking them at first, but slowly getting them used to his presence. The third and fourth months had been the hardest, but the effort had been well worth it. Nearly every deer that regularly came when he called was willing to take a slice of apple from his hand.

Hank sipped his coffee, read his book, and waited. He had been watching these deer since the buck's antlers were still in velvet and the fawn's tan hides were still covered in spots. He knew their habits and their personalities. The six point was always the last to come. The six point was a magnificent specimen, a hunter's dream. He came walking towards the fence with the poise of a king, his widely set antlers a crown upon his head. Hank got up from his chair and with a slice of apple in his hand walked up to the fence. The six point moved forward with the air of a master accepting a gift from a servant. Hank held his breath and willed his heart to slow its beating. The six point reached for the apple. Hank put his free hand into his coat pocket and withdrew it with a fluid and easy motion.

The pistol shot echoed across the creek bottom. Birds took flight, deer scattered and ran, and the six point fell dead to the ground. Hank, adrenaline coursing through his veins, put the pistol back in his pocket, quickly climbed over the fence, hoisted the deer over, and then climbed back to his side of the line.

The Optimist

So, I was sitting in the Road House down there in Rosedale when the little fella came in. I'd been working all morning down south of East Coulee there, so it seemed fair that I stop off at the bar on my way home for a coupla drinks to get the chill out. Besides, you know, I didn't want to miss any of the curling semi-finals. I'm glad I did stop too, otherwise I might have missed what happened to that Saskatoon sweeper.

Anyways, there weren't that many of us at the Road House, just Howard and I at the bar, Blackie bartending, and a coupla the hockey kids from the Dragons over at one of the tables. It was a quiet night ya know, nothing much going on, the weather colder than a bucket of penguin shit and all that. We just watched the curling, drank our beers, and snacked on the peanuts. At least I was, you know how Howard is about them peanuts, convinced that no one's washing their hands after they use the pisser. Anyways, the little fella came into the bar about halfway through the match between the team from Saskatoon and the team from Calgary.

I'd never seen the guy before, so I'm guessing he wasn't from the valley. He wasn't that big, probably only five foot four or so, and he probably weighed only 140 pounds counting his winter coat. He had one of them cherub faces, you know. Didn't look much older than those hockey boys, but the top of his head was as bald as mine, just a fringe of reddish blonde hair on the sides. He was kind of funny looking, but there wasn't really much the poor guy could do. Whether he shaved his head or grew a beard, that kid face would just make him look ridiculous.

Anyways, he came through the door, kind of nodded at the hockey kids like he knew them, and came up to the bar and pounded his hand down to get Blackie's attention. You know how Blackie hates it when people do that eh, so he took his sweet time turning around from the TV. The little fella looked impatient, kind of fidgety and whatnot. When Blackie didn't turn around he slammed his hand down on the bar again. That one really got to Blackie. He turned around and gave the little fella the eye and asked him what he wanted.

"Four shots of Jack Daniels."

Well, that put Blackie's eyebrows higher on his head, but I guess Blackie must have assumed that the little fella was buying for the hockey kids, given how he nodded at them when he came in and all. Now the little guy didn't really seem all that drunk, I mean he walked in straight and tall, but his voice was a little slurred. You know, sounded like he had a mouthful of food, kind of like he was a Newfie or something. Well, Blackie got out the shot glasses and started pouring each full to the rim real careful like, you know how Blackie gets with the imported stuff. The little fella waited until they were all full and then downed them all one after another. Probably took him less than ten seconds to do it, swear to God. Well boy, you better guess that he got all of our attention. We all sat staring at him, and finally I couldn't take the silence anymore.

10

"Jesus buddy," I said, "I ain't ever seen a man drink like that before."

The little fella turned towards me, his face kind of looking all mopey like, and he said, "you'd drink like me if you had what I had."

Well this really got all our attention. So we all leaned in real close and I asked in a quiet voice, "I know it's none of my business, but what is it that you got?"

The little fella, he peered around a bit, looked me right in the eye, and said, "Fifty cents."

The little fella gave out a big horse laugh, I tell you what, he had some of the biggest and whitest teeth I ever saw, and pounded the bar again. I could tell Blackie was not too pleased at this point. You know how pale he is. How easy it is to see when he gets mad. Well, his face was redder than a firetruck. I could see him reaching down under the bar for that butt end of a cue stick he keeps down there to deal with troublemakers. The little fella must have seen it too, because his face got all serious right quick.

"Relax buddy," he said, "my friend Mr. Borden has my tab tonight."

Blackie, still feeling around for his club, answered back rather sharpish, "I don't give a damn about your friend Mr. Borden, nobody drinks on credit here at my bar."

The little fella just gave Blackie a wink, then pulled out his wallet, and laid a hundred dollar bill on the bar. He put his wallet away rather quick, but I saw a flash of yellow when he opened it. Mr. Borden had a lot of friends if you know what I mean. Blackie saw it too because he calmed down again right quick. It was a slow night at the Road House, and even the good nights aren't exactly what you call money makers. So Blackie calmed down right quick and became as polite as if the little fella was the prime minister or something.

"What else will you have," he asked?

"Bring me a Rickard's Red and keep them coming," answered the little fella.

Well, Blackie brought the little fella his beer and he started drinking it rather quick, you know, not chugging it, but not letting the glass hit the bar either. We all kind of watched him for a bit as he went through one and Blackie brought him another.

You could tell that this all had old Howard in quite a twist, so finally he leaned over and said, "so you're some kind of joker, eh?"

The little fella turned towards him with this real serious look on his face, foam all over his upper lip, and said, "I might be, maybe. You ever hear the about the time Bobby figured out his wife was cheating on him?"

We all shook our heads no, and the little fella gave us a flash of his choppers again.

"Well, Bobby was having a drink with his friend Ole, and he says Ole, I don't know what to do, I just figured out that my wife's been cheating on me. Well, Ole puts down his drink and says, hell that's nothing to be upset about, my wife Lena has been sleeping with the guy who drives the ice cream truck for the past ten years. This of course shocks the heck out of Bobby, and he says, Ole, how is it that you've known for the past ten years that the guy who drives the ice cream truck has been sleeping with your wife and have never done anything about it? Well replied Ole, it's not so bad. The wife, she's always nice and cheerful like you wouldn't believe, and my freezer is always full of ice cream sandwiches I never paid for, so you know, seems like a pretty fair trade."

The little fella let out another horse laugh and the three of us with him at the bar all gave an appreciative chuckle, even Howard. It wasn't that good of a joke, but it was better than the crap that Howard usually tells. You know, like the one about the guy with his thumb up his ass so his hamster doesn't escape.

Anyways, after that we all just got back to watching the curling and the little fella stayed quiet, sucking down his beers. He must have been five or so in when he got up to use the bathroom.

"I'm going to leak the lizard," he said.

We all just kind of ignored him, you know. Wasn't really any of our business. No need to make a big production out of it. The little fella hopped off his stool, and maybe it was just me, but he didn't look all that steady on his feet, and headed for the bathroom. None of us really paid attention because it was right then that the Saskatoon sweeper took that fall, you know the one, where he smashed out all his teeth on the stone. Oh boy, you better believe the bar erupted then. Everyone yammering and pointing.

Anyways, right in the middle of it the little fella came back out of the bathroom, and I swear to god, his pecker was just hanging there out of his pants. The whole damn bar went quiet. We all just sat there, trying not to stare, but really not able to look away you know. I don't know how the little fella couldn't of noticed it. The Road House is always colder than a witch's tit, you know, because Blackie is such a cheapskate. Either way he strolled out comfortable as you please, his pecker swinging with every step, sat back on his stool at the bar, and went back to drinking his beer.

Well, we all just looked at each other, no one sure what to do. You know, someone had to say something, but no one wanted to be the one to say it. So, finally after a lot of head gesturing, Howard, he finally takes the bull by the horns.

"Excuse me," he said, "hey buddy, excuse me. Just thought you might like to know that your pecker is hanging out."

The little fella just gave Howard this puzzled look and said, "what?"

Then Howard repeated himself, "I said your dick is hanging out of your pants."

13

Well, the little fella looked down and stared for a bit, then looked back up at Howard and said, "oh, so it is," and then went back to drinking his beer.

Oh boy, you could just tell that it flummoxed the hell out of old Howard. He just kind of sat there for a bit, took a deep breath, then gestured with his hand. "Well, aren't you going to put it away?"

The little fella just smiled again and said, "nah, cheap air conditioning." He then gave off another horse laugh and turned towards Blackie and asked for another beer.

Well, Howard gave a good laugh at that one, and I even gave a little chuckle, but you could tell that Blackie wasn't too pleased one bit. The red was creeping back into his face and he was feeling back under the bar for his club again. The little fella just sat there grinning like an idiot up at Blackie.

"C'mon now," he said, "where's that beer?"

It took Blackie a couple of times to get it out, but he answered, "you want that beer you put your pecker back in your pants. I ain't running that kind of bar."

You could tell Blackie was getting real close to hitting the little fella, but the little fella just grinned, put his pecker back in his pants, pulled out his wallet, and laid another hundred dollar bill on the bar. Blackie was still thinking about hitting him, but those two yellow bills were staring up at him pretty hard, so in the end he just turned and got the little fella his drink.

Well, we all sat pretty quiet after that, just watching the curling, but Blackie kept side eyeing the little guy, you know, to make sure he didn't try any more funny business. His patience was getting pretty thin. You know how much of a temper Blackie has. Anyways, despite being down a sweep the Saskatoon boys were still keeping up pretty well with the Calgary team, and we all got to talking about the likelihood of them pulling off an upset. Blackie of course was pretty bleak about the whole thing, not because he was any fan of Saskatoon, but you know, just because that's the way he is. Blackie was laying it on pretty thick, making us all feel pretty bad about the Calgary team's chances. It really started to get on my nerves.

Finally I got tired of it and I said, "Jesus Blackie, try to be a little more positive, you know, glass half full and all that."

The little fella piped up just then, "I'm a glass half empty kind of guy myself, but only because I drank the first half."

That one really got to Howard. He started hooting and slapping the bar and the little fella gave off another one of his horse laughs. Boy did that ever get to Blackie, he leaned down and got right in the little fella's face. Didn't say anything, just ground his teeth.

The little fella acted like he wasn't there. He just motioned with his arm towards Howard and me and said, "you fellas are all right by me. Barkeep, a round of drinks for my friends."

Blackie backed off and started filling the drinks. Money is money after all. He laid the drinks down in front of Howard and me and I raised mine up to say thanks. Pretty decent of the little guy. Boy-o-boy, you would of thought he was Howard's long lost brother after he bought those drinks. You know how Howard gets when he gets drinking. Thanked the little fella again and again. Told him it was pretty darn nice of him and all. I didn't see the need for such a fuss, you know, it was just a beer, but that's just the way Howard is. Of course old Howard decided that he couldn't be outdone, but we all already had full beers in front of us, so he asked Blackie to bring us all a pull-tab ticket.

The little fella just smiled and waved his hand, "no thank you, never play the things, too damn lucky you know."

Well this really got Howard's attention, and I could even tell Blackie was listening in, though he was trying to pretend that he wasn't.

"What do you mean," asked Howard, "what do you mean you're too lucky?"

15

"Like I said," answered the little fella, "I'm just too lucky."

"Yeah," said Howard, "but wouldn't you want to play the pull tabs then?"

The little fella just pretended that he didn't hear the question. He asked, "any of you have any idea what the odds are of two brown eyed people having a blue eyed kid?"

We all just sat and stared at him a bit, not sure where he was going with all this. Finally Blackie piped up that it depends on the recessive genes each parents got in them and that the chances aren't all that high. Blackie knows a bit about such random things, he's always reading and whatnot when the bar is empty.

"That's right," said the little fella,"that's right, pretty slim. Now what are the chances do you think of two brown eyed people having four blue eyed kids?"

"Pretty slim I guess," said Howard.

"Well there you go," said the little fella, "just like I told you. I'm too damn lucky to be playing the pull tabs."

The little fella gave off another one of his horse laughs. I could tell that Howard wasn't content with the answer, but right then the Calgary boys were throwing their last rock and things got pretty exciting for a bit. It was a hard toss. The Saskatoon team had two rocks close to the center and two more blocking the easy route in, but the Calgary skip threw himself a doozy, curled it right around the guards and landed it right on the button. Won the whole damn thing. We were all cheering and carrying on. It was a beautiful shot. Blackie walked down the bar, high fiving Howard and me as he went. He got down by the little fella, stopped for a second, and must have decided what the hell because he raised his hand for the little fella to give him a high five too.

The little fella just looked at Blackie's hand for a moment, smiled with his big teeth, cocked his arm back, and swung it forward. Right before their two hands hit the little fella put his hand into a fist with the thumb sticking out and tapped the pinky end right on Blackie's palm. Blackie's eyes got real big like, and the little guy, grinning like an idiot, shouted out, "turkey."

The whole bar erupted, even the hockey kids at their table. Blackie turned bright red and just completely lost it. He started screaming and reaching for that club of his under the bar.

"That's it, that's it," he yelled, "get the fuck out of my bar!"

The little fella put his hands up in front of himself and leaned back, but he couldn't get himself to stop laughing. "It's okay," said the little fella, "it's okay. Just a joke."

Oh boy, Blackie really lost it. You know how he gets. He brought that club up and held it up by his head. I thought he was going to whack the little guy. The little fella couldn't seem to get himself to stop laughing, which wasn't helping at all.

"You get the hell out," screamed Blackie, "you get the hell out right now!"

"Okay, okay," said the little fella, "I'll get going. No problem. No need to bash in my head or anything."

The little fella drained the last of his beer and then put it carefully down on the bar, right on top of those two yellow bills there, and then turned and calmly walked out. Acted like nothing was wrong. Blackie watched him go, breathing all heavy. Howard and I didn't say anything, just sat and nursed the beers the little fella had bought us. After about fifteen minutes or so I excused myself to go outside for a smoke.

Out in the parking lot the little fella was sitting in a big green Chevy with his head down on the steering wheel. I felt kinda bad for him getting kicked out like that, so I thought I better go over and make sure he was okay. I walked up to the window and gave it a tap. The little fella bounced right up and started grinning with his big teeth as soon as he saw me. I motioned for him to roll down the window, and he did just a bit, you know, so not too much of the heat would escape. It was pretty damn cold out.

"You all right," I asked?

"Oh yeah, oh yeah sure," he said.

He didn't look okay to me. So I said, "you sure, you look a bit upset if you don't mind me saying."

"No worries at all," said the little fella, "just got a bit of bad news at the hospital today."

"Oh yeah," I said, "what kind of news?"

I knew it was really none of my business, but to be honest with ya, my curiosity was really piqued by now. He was just such a funny acting little fella.

"Oh, it's bad," replied the little fella, "just real bad."

"Yeah," I said.

"Oh yeah. Not good at all," he said.

I waited for him to go on, but he just kind of sat there, grinning away at me. Finally I couldn't take it no more. "So what is it," I asked?

"Well," said the little fella, "well, are you sure you want to hear this?"

"Yes," I said. "I'm sure."

The little fella let his grin fall into a frown. He licked his lips a bit. Looked down at his hands and licked his lips again. "I found out I'm lactose intolerant," he said.

I just stared at him. Here I was expecting him to say that he had cancer or something, and the little bastard was going on about a little thing like that.

"Yep," said the little fella, "lactose intolerant, this is really going to change things. Boy can I tell you, this is really going to change things."

I didn't know what to say. I really just wanted to go back in the bar and be done with the weirdo, but it was obvious that he was pretty drunk, and I felt like I should at least say something.

"Are you sure you're okay to drive," I asked?

"Oh yeah," he said, "I just got to get up to Hanna. Should be no trouble at all."

"You could just go back to Drumheller," I suggested. "Couple of good motels in Drumheller."

"No," said the little fella, "I just got to get to Hanna. Got people waiting for me in Hanna. Have a good night."

The little fella didn't wait for a reply. He put the car in gear, backed up, and headed down the highway. I watched that green Chevy of his until it disappeared into the darkness. He was just such an odd little fella. Never seen anything quite like him before. I tell you though, the real strange thing about all of it. That was that same green Chevy that they pulled out of the Red Deer River last week. You know, down by Dorothy. He was just an odd little fella.

Apple Jacks

You know, when I peruse the Facebook anymore it seems like there's a lot of constant talk about all the terrible things in this world. All of our elected officials are conniving lying bastards, corporations have absolutely no regard for us beyond their ability to make a buck, there are children out there who don't have access to clean drinking water, collectively we are destroying our planet's environment, and god damn Apple Jacks don't taste a damn thing like apples.

Seriously, why are we not talking about this more? The damn cereal is named Apple Jacks. The logo on the front of the box is an obvious, and universally accepted, representation of an apple. But what happens when you shove a big old spoonful in your mouth? Do your taste buds explode with the tart crisp taste of apples? No. All you get is the taste of dry corn meal sweetened by sugar that is made from even more corn. Corn is a pretty amazing plant when you think about all the things we use it for, but it sure as hell is not the same thing as apples.

Now I understand that there is a small matter of marketing. I can understand that Apple Jacks is a much better name for a cereal than Corn Holes, or whatever the hell else they were considering. I also know that Apple Jacks do contain apples, though to such a minute degree that it is pointless to even mention them. You might as well call the damn cereal Yellow #5 Jacks. It's like making a movie where Brad Pitt has a three second cameo, and then putting "starring Brad Pitt" on the poster. What I'm trying to say is that the whole apple thing is pretty much a bunch of bullshit.

I think what really bothers me is how up-front Kellogg's is about it. Hell, for a while their entire marketing campaign was centered around blatantly admitting that the damn cereal tastes nothing like apples. It's one thing to do something dishonest and try to hide it. It's a whole different ball game when you rub people's faces in it. It's like Kellogg's slept with your wife, then called you up at the office to tell you about it, and then asked you to stop by the drug store on your way home to pick them up another box of condoms. This is not the way people show respect for each other.

So this is my question. What the hell America? Why is it that in our modern world with all of our blogs, memes, posts, and tweets, we are still putting up with such an obvious outrageous lie? I mean c'mon. We are the most easily outraged country in the world. We are the people who collectively forced several major corporations to remove a preservative from bread because it could also be found in yoga mats. Never mind that our top scientists told us that there was nothing to be afraid of. That damn preservative had a creepy chemical name and had uses that did not involve putting it in our mouths, so it had to go. Sure, we could have all calmed down, done a little research, and thought to ourselves how cool it is that yoga mats contain something edible, but that is not the way we do it in this country.

Yet, despite our unquenchable social energy to assault every problem, whether it's imaginary or not, we as a society have done nothing to take on the Apple Jacks chicanery. Where the hell is the angry barrage on the Kellogg's website? Where are the posts and reposts? Where are the watchdogs to protect us from all that is wrong? I mean hell, unlike most of the things mentioned at the start of this spiel, this is something that we can actually solve with very little effort. Just a few words and a few clicks. But do we do it? No.

So the next time you post some random crap about all the terrible things going on in the world today, you just remember, Apple Jacks doesn't taste like apples, and that's on you.

Kuku Kane

Do you remember your grandfather, my little Pulelehua?
Back when I lived with him in the old house in Haiku? Do you
remember the stories he would tell you while I rubbed the salve
on the back of his legs to help loosen them after his evening
swim? You would sit in rapt attention, your father's almond
eyes wide in your mother's nut brown face, and listen to him tell
the stories of our people. Your favorites were the stories of how
Maui fished the islands from the sea and how Kamehameha
united all of them under his rule. Do you remember sitting in the
old wooden chair, staring at your grandfather as he laid on his
belly on the couch, his legs on a towel so he wouldn't stain the
cushions? He knew all of our legends by heart. He was a good
man, your grandfather.

I would rub the salve on and leave it to dry. Your
grandfather would sip rum and tell you stories, stopping only to
send you to the kitchen to refill his glass. You would find your
way by touch because all the lights were out. The lights were
always out in those days, our house only lit by the lights of our

neighbors. Your grandfather did the best he could. In those days your grandfather was not a drunk, he did not drink to forget his pain, only to relax himself enough so he could go to bed early. Once upon a time he would not have needed the rum. I would have been enough to relax him. It would have been me beneath his belly instead of the couch. But by that time my charms were already gone, and he had reached an age where his cravings were not what they once were. To be honest my Pulelehua, even then I would have given him whatever it was that he asked. Your grandfather was always a handsome man.

I can still remember the first time I saw him. When he walked into the main office at the sugar plantation. I worked there as a secretary. One of the field bosses had sent him with a message for one of the big haole bosses. He was a magnificent man to behold. Thick black hair hanging down his back. Shoulders like a bull. He worked out in the fields, cutting the cane with a machete. He had taught himself to cut with either hand, so his muscles grew evenly on both sides. I know you must laugh to hear me describe him, for you he was always just an old man, but that was not what he always was, so long ago. In that office he paused to look at me, and I knew he would be the one that I would forever love. He walked away without saying anything. A year later we were married.

Does it bother you, my little one? Does it bother you to think of your grandfather and I so young? Is it so strange to think of your grandfather as the man that I just described? Once I was beautiful, every bit as beautiful as you, but before your grandfather I was helpless, driven forward by a need that I seemed unable to control. When he was young, your grandfather's lusts could not be sated, and for many years after he carried me across the threshold of the house he bought for us in Haiku, our neighbors nightly lullaby was the cries of my ecstasy. Your grandfather was the last of our ancient warriors.

A man of great power, but one with no place in the world in which he found himself.

Your grandfather would drink the rum so he could fall asleep early. He would awaken before dawn to sneak to the houses of the haoles to steal the fruits of our islands from their trees. Guava, papaya, and mango. Your grandfather never considered it stealing, for in his mind the bounty of the islands belonged to all, just as it had in the days when our people ruled themselves. He never stole the coconuts, for they were always easy to come by. The fruit was for his stand on the Hana Highway, where he would mix the fruit juice with the juice from the sugarcane and sell it to the haole tourists as they passed through packed in their rented cars with sunburnt faces. They'd hand him their money, and he would smile and tip his head.

Your parents often sent you to us in those days. Back when you lived in Lahaina, the city once ruled by kings, now ruled by the dollars of the haole tourists. Your parents wanted time to be alone. They wanted time to try and make you a brother or a sister, though neither ever came. By then they could no longer relax. Relax like they could when the flames of their passion were still high. Relax like the time they brought you into this world. It was obvious even then what was going to happen, but we never said a thing. The reasons changed, but still you came. Your grandfather and I never minded. We enjoyed having you with us.

Your grandfather was always strong. Even in the twilight of his years, when the world had worn him down, and made his shoulders slump. He would climb the fruit trees in the morning and go swimming in the ocean every evening. Your grandfather could swim like a dolphin. When he still had hair, I would spend the evenings combing it for him, five hundred strokes with my brush, and a dozen promises never to tell anyone that I did it. I loved the feeling of his hair in my hands. Thick and strong like him. When his hair started coming out with the brush strokes, he had me shave him bald, so that it would be his choice, instead of the way of the world. Do you remember helping me when you were young? Do you remember putting the foam on his scalp, and then clearing it off with the razor that I never replaced because it never wore out?

Your grandfather hated the haoles, though I do not have to tell you that. Everyone on the island knows how he hated them. He hated their arrogance and their belief that everything has a price. He hated the big houses that they threw across the hills, and the highways they laid down to make their invasion easier. Most of all he hated the mocking way that they called themselves local, though their ancestors were all buried on the mainland far away. It hurt him a great deal to have to serve them as he did. To welcome them and their money as they slowly destroyed the Hawaii that we had known. Your grandfather was a proud man. He never let it show. He kept his head held high. He never fell into despair like so many others. He knew he was fighting a battle he could not win, but he refused to ever give up.

Do you know how much your grandfather loved you Pulelehua? When your mother married he refused to talk to her, because she married an outsider. Your father was born on this island, but to your grandfather he would always be Chinese. It did not help that your father worked for the big resorts on the west side of the island. Your grandfather was too proud. He did not talk to your mother for three years. I had to sneak away to see her. When you were born I convinced your mother to take you to him. A brown grub wrapped tightly in a pink blanket. An offering for peace. Your grandfather would not change his opinions, but from then on he kept the peace to keep you in our lives.

Do you remember helping me rub the salve on to his legs? The feeling of the countless tiny white scars beneath your fingertips? You helped me once or twice, but I could tell that

28

you didn't like it. Your head filled with too many questions that you knew you couldn't ask. Getting the rum and listening to the stories was a much better job for you. Do you remember when he took us up to Haleakala? How we had to beg him to take us up to see the snow? Your grandfather never liked to travel. If he never left home, he would not have to face how the world had changed. Did you know that he never left Maui once in his life? For you he would do anything, and so we loaded up in his rusty little pickup, and drove up to the top. He only wore shorts and a t-shirt, and we knew that he would be cold, but he would not listen. His teeth chattered for an hour as you and I played, but he never once complained.

Your grandfather never wanted to work along the highway. It nearly killed him the day that they fired him from the plantation. The day they replaced all the men with machines. They kicked him out with an extra two weeks pay, and not even a handshake to thank him for his years. Your grandfather had not minded working on the plantation. In his mind it was better to work for the haoles that had brought the sugar, then the haoles that only brought themselves and their suitcases full of cash. At least the one allowed a man to still work with his pride intact. Perhaps if your mother had not been in high school at the time, perhaps then he would have let himself slip into despair like so many of our friends and neighbors, but your grandfather was a stubborn man, and for his family he would do what he had to do. Even if it left him a shrunken husk of what he once was. The man who could with just a glance make me feel the moisture on my thighs.

Do you remember the one time he got angry with you? Do you my little Pulelehua? The day you came to visit and told of how you and your friends had thrown glass bottles out the bus windows at a haole walking along the road. Do you remember how he ranted? Do you remember how he raved? He took you by the arm and shook you, and for the first time he made me feel afraid. "Do not do such things," he yelled, "don't ever do it again. Don't waste your time on such things that do nothing. You are only masturbating your anger." Of course that was before he himself started spitting in the drinks. By then you did not come around as much, your time taken up between the two households of your parents. He missed you terribly.

Did you know that he used to spit in the haoles' drinks? He started after he fell out of the mango tree, and he stopped being the man that you remembered. His stand along the Hana Highway was small. Just rough boards nailed together, decorated with bamboo because it was what the haoles expected it to look like. He would bring the cane juice in the old rum bottles. I'd squeeze the sugar cane here each night. The sugar cane came from the plantation, payment for a debt that was never paid. He would put the freshly cut fruit slices in the cane juice and mix them with a blender that ran off an old gas generator that your Uncle Kawika found in the dump and fixed up.

Your grandfather was clever how he did it, how he spit into the haoles' drinks. Your grandfather was too quick and sly, though I hated that he took the risk. Only once did a haole catch him. The man grew red in the face and started yelling. Your grandfather just smiled, slapped him on the shoulder, and told him that it was the customary island way amongst friends. The man thanked him and even paid a little extra. Your grandfather loved to tell that story. It was one of the few things that could make him laugh after you had gone.

It was a bad day the day he fell from the mango tree, when the haoles found him in the morning, stretched out beneath the leaves. He lay with a fractured skull, amongst the fallen over ripened fruit. His body healed, as I knew it would, but his mind after that was never quite the same. He lost a lot of what he was. You didn't come around anymore by then my Pulelehua. You didn't have to hear our neighbors whisper that he was a thief. Your parents had taken you to Honolulu, to try and start

30

again. He was still quick, but his memory turned to mush, and he didn't tell the stories anymore. After that he always bought the fruit, and made less money than he did before.

After the stand along the highway closed, your grandfather spent most of his time fishing with your Uncle Kawika down on the shore. He collected his checks from the government on the mainland. I would hide the envelope and cash them myself so he would never have to see. It was never enough, and it was then that I took the job in Kahului, answering phones for a lawyer who had at times been more than friends with your mother. It was the first time that I had worked since the day your grandfather carried me across the threshold of our house in Haiku. It filled him with shame, and he at last gave in and let the rum carry him away. I blame the bad influence of your Uncle Kawika and his brood. They used to walk the beaches every night and beat up haoles that set up tents. Your grandfather never joined them, but only because he had already drank himself to sleep. His retirement did not last long. The night when he did not come back from his evening swim, I wasn't that surprised.

God how I loved your grandfather. Even after the world had whittled him down to just a nub of what he once had been. His body was swept out to sea, but his spirit died the day the stand closed and he could no longer make his own way. The stand did not last long after they added the convenience store to the gas station in Paia. The haoles would stop to buy the same cans of Koka and bags of chips that they could buy at home, and then no longer had any reason to stop along the highway as they once did. Soon after a man from the state came and told your grandfather that if he was going to run the stand, he'd need licenses and permits. Twenty years of working without, but the past did not matter. Your grandfather never worked the stand again.

When he left the stand along the highway for the last time, your grandfather took his knife, the sharp knife that he used to slice the fruit, and for the final time gave himself a small cut across the back of his leg. A small cut, just as he had done at the end of every day for the twenty years that he had worked at the stand. Do you remember your grandfather Pulelehua? Do you remember who he was?

Rescued

They found the man at eight in the morning. He was sitting
in the remains of an eighty year old shack that was half collapsed
at the bottom of the draw. The boards were gray and curved
with blue sky peeking through. The shack leaned as though it
was a drunk who had been refused last call, a balancing act that
amazingly never falls. The man sat in the corner most protected
from the wind, his little brown mutt lying on his lap. The dog
eyed the policeman, local neighbors, and volunteer firemen
warily. The man said nothing, his breath steaming, as he stood
and walked with them out into the sunshine that had burned
away the fog.

The rusty pickup sat in a snow drift more than three miles
away on the ridge far out of sight. Its back end filled with cans
and its floorboards covered with bottles. It sat in the middle of a
blanket of freshly fallen snow. A virgin covering only marred
by the tire tracks and the footsteps of the searchers, hiding all

evidence of those who had crossed before. The group started walking back towards the pickup.

The policeman beamed at one of the volunteer firemen.

"That was brilliant sounding the siren. I don't think we would have ever found him if it wasn't for his dog."

The volunteer fireman smiled and nodded in acknowledgement, his face red and his breathing hard as they climbed back up the hill.

"I'm just glad everything turned out alright."

The policeman looked at the man struggling through the snow with his rescuers. The man said nothing as he walked. No gratitude or grace. He simply reached into his coat pocket and offered each a pull from a bottle only a quarter full.

Drinks

There was a resounding click when the phone was hung up. The farmer's wife walked into the sitting room and sat in her overstuffed chair. The farmer didn't look up from his newspaper, but he knew by the sounds of her footsteps, and the long sigh when she sat down, that it wasn't good news.

"Well Rob, that was Mariel."

"Hmmmmm." The farmer knew it was better to show that he was listening. Otherwise he would be forced to put down the newspaper.

"The Johnsons aren't going to be able to make it over for drinks this evening. They have a heifer that looks like she's going to calve tonight and they don't want to get too far from home until she does."

"Hmmmmm."

"Are you listening to me?"

The farmer let out his own sigh, folded the paper, put it on the table next to his chair, and looked up at his wife. "Of course I'm listening Jenny. I just don't know what you want me to do about it. If they have a heifer calving they have a heifer calving. That's just the way it is."

"I know. I was just looking forward to a little socializing. We haven't really had much of a chance since New Year's."

The farmer grunted and picked back up his newspaper. "We'll get together with the Johnson's soon. Can't hardly blame them for a narrow hipped heifer."

The wife sat in her chair and stared at nothing for a bit before giving out another weary sigh. She got up and paced the room a few times before going into the kitchen. The farmer could hear her open the fridge, rattle around a bit, close the fridge, open the cupboard, close the cupboard, and open a different cupboard. She came back into the sitting room and rearranged several of the knick knacks on the mantle before taking the poker to unnecessarily poke at the logs in the fire. The farmer sighed, put down his newspaper again, and got up.

"I better feed the cows before it gets dark. It's already late."

The wife nodded without looking away from the fire. The farmer put on his boots, coat, and cap and walked out the door. There would be no peace in the house for a little while. The yard was covered in a thin layer of snow and each footstep was accompanied by a crunch. The sun was already below the horizon and everything was covered in shadows. The farmer walked across the yard, grabbed the pitchfork, and began to fill the feed bunk with hay. It was automatic work, something he did every morning and evening during the winter.

In truth, the farmer was disappointed about the whole thing as well. He didn't much like the Johnsons, Henry was a dullard and Mariel used ten words where just one would suffice, but he did enjoy the drinks. Jenny wasn't keen on him drinking when not socializing. He did feel bad for his wife. The farmer was very content with his solitary life, but his wife had grown up in town. Even after thirty years she still often found the isolation unsettling.

The hay bunks were full. The farmer put down the pitchfork and watched the two old dairy cows eat. One was a guernsey, her hide red and white. The other was a holstein, her body white and black. The farmer kept them for the fresh milk they provided. A queer idea formed in the farmer's head. It was a strange idea. The kind of idea that the mind normally quashes as ridiculous but given the right stimulus can escape before it's fully analyzed.

"Excuse me ladies," said the farmer, "but would the two of you be interested in coming inside for some drinks?"

The two cows stopped eating and looked at him quizzically. "Pardon?" asked the holstein.

"Would you be interested in joining me and the missus inside for a couple of drinks?"

"We've never been allowed inside the house before," stated the guernsey.

"I know it's a bit unusual, but we'd be more than pleased if you'd join us."

The two cows conferred quietly for a moment. The farmer stood politely and pretended not to listen in. The holstein was the one that answered. "We would be delighted to join you."

"Great," said the farmer.

The farmer opened the gate to the cow pen and the three walked across the yard. The farmer leading and the two cows following. The farmer walked into the house and yelled down the hallway. "Jenny. Jenny, honey. We have company."

The wife came down the hallway, smiling as the farmer took off his coat and hat. "Who is it? Did the Johnson's come after......" She turned the corner and saw the two cows sniffing by the doorway. "Rob, the cows are out."

"I know. I've invited them to join us for a drink."

The wife's face fell, but she quickly covered it up with a smile just as big, if not as sincere. "Oh." The wife had always been a good hostess and she wasn't about to let the unexpected cause a deviation in her trend. She turned and smiled at the cows. "Welcome to our home."

"Thank you," said the holstein.

"Delighted," said the guernsey.

"Ladies, please wipe your feet and follow me into the sitting room," said the farmer.

The two cows dutifully wiped their four feet on the mat and walked into the house. They followed the farmer down the hallway, their hooves clicking on the hardwood floors, careful not to brush any of the pictures off the walls.

"You have a lovely home," said the guernsey.

"Thank you," said the wife.

While the wife led the cows into the sitting room the farmer went into the kitchen to mix some drinks. The wife stood politely while the cows examined the knick knacks on the mantle and the phonograph in the corner with great interest, their tails swishing amiably, chewing their cuds.

"What a lovely rug," said the holstein.

"Thank you," said the wife, "it was my grandmother's."

"We don't have rugs in the barn," said the guernsey, "we just have straw."

The holstein was quick to cover her friend's social faux pas. But it's very clean straw."

"It sounds very nice," said the wife.

The farmer walked in carrying a tray holding a bottle of scotch, a bucket of ice, two snifters, and two wine glasses. He set it carefully on the coffee table. "Here are the drinks," said the farmer. "I've brought two wine glasses for your hooves."

"How very thoughtful," replied the holstein.

"Please be seated," said the farmer.

"Seated?" asked the holstein.

"What do you mean?" questioned the guernsey.

The farmer looked at the wife, and the wife looked at the farmer. "Seated," said the farmer, "like this." The farmer sat down in his chair and the wife did the same in hers. The two cows watched with great interest.

"How quaint," said the guernsey.

"We usually just lie down," explained the holstein.

The two cows maneuvered themselves and clumsily laid their hindquarters on the couch. It was obvious that it was a very new experience for them and the farmer and his wife politely hid their smiles of amusement. There was a little confusion over what to do with their tails and how to most comfortably position their large ponderous bags and udders, but finally they got themselves settled.

"Very comfortable," said the holstein.

The wife smiled politely and the farmer leaned forward and uncorked the bottle. "Would you like ice in your drinks?" he asked the cows.

"Yes please," said the holstein.

"No thank you," said the guernsey.

The farmer poured four generous glasses of scotch and passed them out, starting with the two guests. With drinks in hand or hoof everyone settled back in their respective seats and an awkward silence filled the room. Everyone took polite sips of their drinks, no one quite sure what to say.

The holstein was a good enough guest to break the silence. "This is a very fine scotch."

"Yes it is," replied the farmer, "it's a double malt."

The room descended back into uncomfortable silence. The cows feeling nervous, finished their drinks quite quickly. The farmer and his wife, to be polite, drank their own down as well, though it was a much faster pace than they were used to.

"Would you like another?" asked the farmer.

"Indeed," quipped the guernsey.

"Why not," said the holstein.

The farmer refilled the glasses and passed them out again. Both cows seemed to greatly enjoy their drinks.

"How has everything been out in the barnyard?" asked the wife, trying to start a conversation.

"It's been fine," stated the holstein.

"Just a few things," said the guernsey.

"Like what?" questioned the wife.

"Oh nothing," said the holstein, "nothing important."

"It's no problem," said the wife, "please tell us."

The holstein looked embarrassed. "It's just a silly little thing."

"Nonsense," said the guernsey. She turned her great head to the farmer. "It would just be nice if you warmed your hands before you milked us sir."

"Pardon?" asked the farmer.

"Your hands sir," replied the holstein, "they're just very cold on our udders."

The two cows sat looking serious. The wife smiled and giggled slightly behind her hand. The farmer looked befuddled.

"Of course," said the farmer. "I'll make sure my hands are warm from now on. My apologies for not realizing the problem sooner."

"Don't worry about it," said the guernsey.

"There is another thing," said the holstein, feeling braver at the polite response.

"What is it?" asked the farmer.

"Well," said the holstein, "it is such a silly thing I feel embarrassed even bringing it up."

"No, please do," said the wife.

"It is such a little thing, "said the holstein, "but it would mean the world to me if you could milk me first every now and again."

"Pardon?" asked the farmer.

"Well sir," said the holstein, "you see, every time you milk us you always milk Della first. I just think it would be nice if you milked me first every now and again."

40

"Who's Della?" asked the wife.

"I'm Della," answered the guernsey.

The wife blushed. "I've been calling you Clover."

"I know," said the guernsey, "I find it very strange."

"My apologies," said the wife in a most apologetic tone.

"Don't worry about it," said the holstein.

"Easy for you to say Daisy," said the guernsey, "she's been getting your name right."

"I'll always call you by the right name from now on," said the wife.

"Thank you," said the guernsey.

Uncomfortable silence descended on the room again. The two cows finished their drinks and the farmer reached forward and refilled their glasses again.

"Most grateful," said the guernsey.

"Never a finer host," said the holstein.

The farmer's wife leaned forward, sat back, and then leaned forward again. "I have a question," she said giving a nervous giggle, "but I'm afraid it might be a little personal."

The guernsey rolled her eyes, but the holstein leaned forward and laid her hoof on the wife's hand in a friendly manner. "Please feel free to ask anything dear."

"Well," said the wife, giggling once again. "I....I was just wondering if you enjoyed it when you got milked?"

The farmer's face turned red but the two cows looked at each other with their faces bent in bovine approximations of a smile.

"Do you want to answer this one?" asked the holstein.

"No I think you better," replied the guernsey.

The holstein turned back to the wife, placing her hoof once again back on top of the wife's hand. "It feels wonderful."

"Best part of the day," quipped the guernsey.

The farmer's face grew a brighter shade of red.

"You see," said the holstein, letting out a cowish giggle of her own. "Our bags fill up with so much milk that it begins to hurt. Getting milked is a great relief to us."

"Especially when it's done by a man with the skills of your husband," slurred the guernsey, leaning forward and giving an exaggerated wink.

The farmer drank the rest of his glass in a single pull and bent down to fill himself another. His face was quite flushed and his wife smirked as he avoided looking anyone in the eye. "We're out of ice," stammered the farmer.

"Please let me get that," offered the holstein.

"Oh no, please stay seated," answered the wife, "you're our guests."

"No I insist," replied the holstein in a volume one decibel above appropriate. The wife relented and the holstein picked up the ice bucket and walked unsteadily into the kitchen.

The guernsey helped herself to another glass of scotch and took it down in a single swallow. She sat swaying tipsily from side to side, her slightly unfocused eyes tracking across the items in the room until they fell on the phonograph in the corner. "Would it be possible to play some music?" asked the guernsey.

The farmer looked at the wife and the wife looked at the farmer. "I guess that would be all right," said the wife as she rose up from her chair.

"Make it something jaunty," slurred the guernsey. Music filled the house and the guernsey's tail began to swish, though not quite in tune with the song. "This makes me want to dance."

"I didn't know cows danced," said the farmer.

"Of course we dance," bellowed the guernsey raising her bulky body from the couch, her movements jerky and clumsy looking. The great red and white cow began hopping from one side to the other, kicking her hooves up into the air. Each landing was met with a resounding crash that shook the entire house. The knick knacks on the mantle rattled and fell to the floor. The wife's eyes grew wide in horror, but her good hospitality silenced any protests before they could begin.

The holstein came back from the kitchen with the ice. Her gait and stance unsteady. Her face had a concerned look on it. "Here is the ice," she said to the farmer, oblivious to the tragedy of dancing being carried out by her comrade.

"What is it?" asked the farmer, noticing the strange look on the holstein's gentle face.

"When I was getting the ice," answered the holstein, "I noticed all sorts of neatly wrapped white packages in the freezer. I don't know why, but they made me feel very uncomfortable."

The farmer looked at the wife and the wife looked at the farmer. "It's nothing," said the farmer. "Don't worry about it."

"It just seemed very strange," slurred the holstein.

The big clock on the wall began to chime the hour.

"Look at the time," said the farmer.

"Yes," said the wife, cutting off the phonograph, "we hate to end the party, but we really must go to bed."

The guernsey looked disappointed, but the holstein nodded her head with exaggerated care. "Of course, of course. It was very nice of you to have us in."

"We'll have to do it again soon," slurred the guernsey.

"Let me show you out," said the farmer.

"A gentleman and a good milker," blurted the guernsey winking again at the wife, "a very fine catch for you."

The farmer led the cows down the hallway, their bodies swaying more than normal and their tails swishing wildly, knocking pictures off the walls. He put on his boots, led the cows outside, put them back into their pen, and shut the gate.

"Good night sir," mumbled the holstein.

"See you in the morning," purred the guernsey, in a poorly done enticing tone, "we'll look forward to the milking." The two cows erupted into barely stifled giggles.

"Sleep well," replied the farmer, glad the night hid his blushing face.

The farmer walked back into the house and found his wife cleaning a fairly sizable cow pie off her grandmother's rug.

"Well, that was a mistake," said the farmer.

"Obviously," said the wife. "I don't know what you were thinking inviting them in."

"It wasn't that bad," replied the farmer.

"That's your opinion," said the wife.

"Well," replied the farmer, "you have to admit, they both had better manners than the horse."

The Trap

Gary sat at the bus stop and waited. The weather was chilly. It was just cold enough to make being outside uncomfortable without a coat. Gary had forgotten his coat at the office. The bus was twenty minutes late, or at least it seemed that way. Gary would normally know for certain, but he had forgotten his watch, the one his father had given him, on the nightstand that morning. The wind picked up and he shivered. Gary considered going back to the office for his coat but knew as soon as he left the bus would arrive. It didn't really matter. Soon he would be home.

A plumpish woman in her mid-thirties walked up and sat on the other side of the bench. She wore a jacket over scrubs, suggesting she was a nurse. Gary nodded politely to her and then paid her no mind. Soon the number eight bus would arrive and Gary would ride it five stops and then walk two blocks to his little green house with the blue door. Martha would have dinner ready, she had said it would be pork chops tonight. After dinner the boys would do their homework while he watched television and read the paper. He'd check over the boys' work and then read David a bedtime story. David was the only one who still wanted bedtime stories. The other two were too old. Gary wished they were young again. He would miss the ritual when David got too old.

It had been a good day at the office. He had found the problem with the Myers account with little fuss, just a few little bookkeeping mistakes. Everyone had been impressed. Problems with the Myers account usually took days to unravel. Mr. Ricketts had brought Gary into his office to congratulate him and hint that advancement to associate would soon be in the picture. Gary hoped it was true. The extra money would be a nice thing for the family. A new car, no more riding the bus, new kitchen appliances for Martha, vacations to Miami.

Gary's brain paused mid-thought. Miami didn't seem right. They already did annual vacations to Miami. The family had been doing them since he made associate. Acapulco was the right place. They were going to go to Acapulco when he made partner. Was that right? Gary was sure he had already been to Acapulco. He could see the blue ocean and white beaches. Something wasn't right. When was the last time David had wanted a bedtime story? Gary looked at his hands. The skin looked like paper and the joints were swollen with arthritis. They didn't look right. They didn't look like his hands.

"Mr. Daly, would you like to come inside with me?"

Gary looked at the nurse sitting next to him on the bench. She was smiling. She seemed familiar though he'd never seen her before. Gary tried to remember what he was doing on the bench but couldn't. It was cold, too cold to be out without a coat. Gary nodded and the nurse helped him stand and walked him back up the sidewalk to the door of the big brick building behind them. His joints felt stiff and his back would not straighten out all the way. Inside the building it was warm and pleasant. A second nurse sat behind a desk. She looked up at the first nurse.

"Catch another one?"

"Yep."

The two nurses smiled at each other. Gary smiled too. It seemed impolite not to.

A Knight In Repose

He lies in his bed in silent shadows, surrounded by the vast emptiness of the room about him. The wind lightly brushes trees outside his window, caressing them like lovers, unseen in the moonless dark. Things are so still that he can hear the sound of time slowly marching forward into the dawn. He lays in bed unarmored and naked. Alone and unprotected from the terrors of the night.

He waits for sleep to overtake him. For the dark and silent world to disappear and be replaced in an instant by a new morning shining bright. He unfetters his mind from its leashes. He lets his thoughts break free from his control to wander aimlessly across the landscape of his psyche. He knows that it must be done. A mind held in rigid control can never relax and fall into blissful sleep. If one must direct everything, then they must be cognizant at all times. One has to learn to let go. It is the only way to survive. The only way to be happy.

The thoughts come, creeping up the shore, an oncoming tide, each wave a little higher than the last. Once he would have struggled against the rising waters. Fought to break their hold and wade back to shore. He knows better now. He knows that nothing can be battered by the waves and last forever. It is better to float with the current and let it carry him where it may. It is better to expend his energies on beasts that he can actually fight. These are but memories. Ghosts from the past. They can only hurt him if he chooses to let them hurt him.

"I want to take this slow. I don't want this to be like the others."

He sits and holds her hand, long delicate fingers wrapped in his. He looks into her eyes, the color of the ocean on a stormy day. Feelings bubble through him that he has never felt before. A strange longing that pushes him forward. He gives her hand a squeeze and smiles. She smiles back and then looks away. Seeing things that only she can see. They sit for a while and watch the world flow past in silence. He never once feels uncomfortable.

Nothing but electrical impulses and chemical reactions. Random bursts of static that light up old thoughts and bring them back into crystal clarity. If he lets himself, he can remember everything as though no time has passed. If he allows it, he can live it all again. He has watched all the scenes a hundred times before. Once he obsessed about them. Searching for ways he could have done better. Wishing he could go back and change the frozen world of the past. Not now. Now he accepts them for what they are and waits for them to pass like sudden showers on summer days.

"I'm sorry."

"I'm sorry too."

It ended like it started. Looking into her eyes. Holding her close one last time and then walking back to his car and driving away. The trees golden and dropping leaves. A year ago they seemed so beautiful. Now they just seem dead. He only makes it three blocks before he has to pull over so he can cry. The tears fall freely and wet his cheeks. There is no one to talk to. There is no one who can understand.

"I never want to see you again."

He has been sent away. A monster now shunned by those he once called friends. All gone. All lost. The sound of music and of singing. A man with glasses playing a guitar as they sit around and sing songs written in old notebooks. He sits amongst them and sings as loud as all the rest. His voice off key but beautiful in his ears. Beautiful in its joys. No worries, no concerns, but a nagging fear that it is all just temporary. The problems have not been solved, just ignored.

So many good memories. So much bittersweet. The softness of her skin beneath his fingers. The look of childlike joy upon her face when she sees him come in the door. The feeling of holding her close at the moment she falls asleep. The tension that holds her tight suddenly slipping away into peaceful bliss. The laughter. Church bells in a morning meadow filled with dew. A contentment with the world with all its trials and tribulations that he has never felt before. So much that once made him smile.

"Anxiety."

Anxiety. Just a single word. Anxiety. Just a solitary hint to explain the horrors that he sees. The ocean eyes, once alive and dancing, sinking back behind the windows of her outer shell. He watches a drowning person slowly slip below the waters. Growing distant and less distinct, and then disappearing into the murky depths. He can do nothing. Just watch as she slips away and struggle to try and understand what is happening.

"I've never tried this before. Once it happens I never get it back."

He had been a boy raised on stories of heroes. People who marched off to battle to defend what they held dear. People who fought even when they knew they were going to lose. People who were not afraid to sacrifice themselves for others. It had never really been a choice. He had always wanted to be a hero, and heroes never run away. In the stories the heroes always win.

"Come back. Please come back," he wants to yell.

Sometimes she would come back, and it would be like it had been before. For a moment, but only for a moment, and then the walls would be rebuilt, and she'd be gone again. A living breathing shell.

"I tremble like a little dog. It's something that I've always done."

The feeling of her shivering as they lay together in her bed. The silent struggle as she retreats to a place he does not understand and where he cannot follow. She fights. She fights hard. He can see it etched in her face. She tries for him where she has never tried before. He tries his best to help, but there is nothing he can do. Each time she comes back she is a little weaker. Each time he knows that he has lost a little more. In the darkness, between the battles, they cling in desperation. Both wishing for the sunlight of better days.

"You have a lot of gray hairs. You didn't have them last month."

The barber is observant. The toll has moved beyond the mind. He can see worry in the barber's eyes. He pays for the haircut and says nothing.

"I don't know why this happens to me."

He holds her close and tries to give what comfort he can. He looks into her ocean eyes, filled with unshed tears.

"What is the one thing that you want most?"

"I want to feel love."

He wants to grab her. He wants to shake her. He wants to yell out loud that it's right here in front of her. That she already has it. But he does not. He knows there is nothing he can do though he still keeps trying when he finds the strength. She expects it all to just go away. For someone to come along and for it all to float away in the wind as though it never was. He has failed to do this, so he is not the one. He holds her as she cries and shakes.

"You don't know what I'm thinking. You can't understand how I feel."

He lets her go because it's what she wants. He lets her go because he is tired. He lets her go because he can no longer watch her be in pain. He lets her go because there is nothing he can do.

"I've known her since college and I've never seen her have a crush like that."

He came back because he loved her. He came back because he cared. He came back because he had learned what could be done. He came back because he did not want to leave her in that place all alone. That place she disappeared to. He knew he could not fight her battles, but he knew how she could. He came back because he hoped. He hoped that the woman that he loved was more than just a dream, more than just a mirage of a possibility. He came back because it was the right thing to do. You can't fight such battles alone.

Euphoria and worry, all bound together in a terrible web with no escape. Feelings that have never been felt before, a high he once thought impossible to reach. But he cannot relax. The truth nibbles at the back of his mind. It is not real. It is just an illusion. A magician's trick waiting for the flutter of the wind to signal that the show is at an end. All he wants is to bask within the sun. All he wants is to have it all be as it once was. But you must go forward and never back, and the right thing is rarely what you want.

"I want to talk to you about your anxiety."

"I want to talk to you about what happened between us."

"I want to talk to you...."

"I want to talk......"

"I want...."

"I want...."

He did the right thing. He could have done it better, but he did the right thing. A mantra repeated again and again in his own head. You can't live your life split in twain. You cannot sit and watch a loved one struggle with the lock if you know the location of the key. You have to try, even if it means the end of your hopes and dreams. Even if you become the monster. The beast forced out of the sunny lands.

"I don't want to talk about it. Talking about it only makes it worse."

"You don't know how I'm feeling. So don't act like you do."

"I don't want to talk about this anymore."

"I don't want to talk..."

"I don't want..."

"I don't....."

"What is wrong?"

"When you're around I'm fine, but when you're gone all I feel is anxiety. I don't want to do this anymore."

"All I feel is anxiety."

"I feel anxiety."

"Anxiety."

"Anxiety."

A man lays and trembles, swept up in the storm. It would be so easy to let it carry him out to sea once again. It would be so easy to let it all come back. It would be so easy to have imaginary conversations where two people talk with each other. So much better than the reality of one person talking at the other while the other sits in silence and disappears into their mind. It would be so easy to imagine that just one right word or phrase could change everything like magic, and the curtain would be drawn back and the darkness in the kingdom would be shown for all to see. It is all so much easier in the fantasy. So much nicer than this world.

He had to try. He had to try his best. He did the right thing. He has to believe it was worth the cost. Even if he failed, he had to try. No matter what else it was the right thing to do. Say it. Believe it. No matter what else it was the right thing to do. Why couldn't she understand how it tore him apart? Why couldn't she understand how much he cared? Why couldn't she see what he saw? Is it better to hide in the fortress of your mind? Is it a better life to never look for the light of day? Was all he did and tried to do the wrong thing? Is he truly the monster that in her eyes he's become? If all of life is just perceptions then who has the truest view?

"Anxiety."

"She has never told anyone as much as you."

"Anxiety."

A single hated word. A reason without reason. Shaking in the dark. Fearing to go away. Knowing that when he comes back all will just be terror instead of smiles. All alone. No one to listen. No one to understand. No one to hold him tight and tell him it will be okay. No one to shelter him from fears or caress him until the break of day.

Who knows at what point the storm ends. When the stage finally goes to black. But the knight awakens with light in his eye as he does each morning, washed back up on the sandy shore. Birds sing, flowers open, and all is well again. He dons his armor and goes forth, ready to face the day, but knowing that he'll have to fight once more, when he lays his head to rest again.

Judgment Day

George smiled as he put his candy bar and can of pop on the counter.

"I'm giving you my bike Ed. You've always liked it and I want you to have it. I put it on your porch."

Ed scowled at his friend across the counter.

"What the hell are you doing George? For god sakes, you have a doctorate in chemistry."

"I don't see what that has to do with anything."

"It's just that it doesn't make any sense."

"Look, if you want to know more about chemistry you'd talk to me right?"

"Yeah."

"If you have a leaky pipe you call a plumber. If you have a faulty switch you call an electrician. If you need a foundation laid you call a contractor."

"So?"

"So you have faith that all these people know about something better than you. That's all this is, faith in someone who knows better."

George continued smiling and Ed continued scowling as he rang up George's purchases.

"I don't know. It just seems odd for God to pick May 22, 2011."

"Would any date seem less odd?"

Ed sighed.

"Probably not."

"You should come. Pastor Matthews is having us meet at the church at eight this evening to start praying. It's not too late to seek redemption."

Part of Ed wanted to shake his friend and call him an idiot, or laugh, or punch George in his self-righteous face.

"Thanks, but no. I have lots of things I need to get done."

George took his change and walked toward the door. As he opened it he turned back.

"I'm going to miss you Ed. You're a good egg."

Ed let his scowl relax.

"If you wouldn't mind, say a few prayers for me George."

"No problem Ed."

"See you later."

George didn't hear. He was already out the door, walking up the street, whistling.

Ed closed the grocery store at six and went home. George's bicycle sat on his porch. He ate dinner alone in front of the television and fell asleep in his chair thinking of his friend praying with the rest of the fools at the church with its padded pews and grape juice instead of wine. The next day he mowed the lawn, trimmed his hedges, and watched Sunday Night Football by himself. On Monday morning he reopened the grocery store promptly at eight.

George was the first customer to arrive. He walked in whistling and got a gallon of milk from the cooler and brought it to the counter. Ed stared at George for a moment but said nothing.

"There was no milk in the house."

Ed nodded, rang up the purchase, and handed George his change. George started to leave.

"Hey George."

George turned with his hand on the door and a smile on his face.

"Yeah."

"You forgot your bike on my porch the other day."

"I was wondering where I left it. Thanks Ed."

"See you later George."

"See you later."

George walked out the door whistling.

The Commodity

Sam puts down the book he is reading and tries to doze for a few hours, but the constant drip of water from the pipe along the ceiling onto the concrete floor is too distracting. In his head he notes each drip, about one every three seconds, and tries counting them like the sheep his mother had told him to count when he was a child. Sam reaches six hundred and thirty-seven plops before he gives up. It would do no good, he is bored, not tired. He sleeps a lot more than he used to. A part of him, a part from the past, still twinges with guilt when he thinks of how much he sleeps. It doesn't really matter. It's not like he has anywhere to go. His mind wanders.

"What are you doing here in Mexico?"

"Your government trades a lot of corn futures. My company wants to be their broker."

"So you are a commodities trader?"

"Yes."

"Good my friend, then you can understand my business. I also trade commodities."

Price ceiling, price floor, trend lines, and Fibonacci sequences. Candle-bar charts with forty-day moving averages climbing and falling. Sell high and buy low. Crop reports each month and daily news updates. Rainfall delays planting in Iowa. Increased exports to China. Funds increasing their long positions. Countless factors both fundamental and technical. Organize and prioritize. Assign importance and make a decision. Get in or get out. Play ball or go home. Winning is easy. Just leave with more than you arrived with. If you want big profits you have to risk big losses. Don't get greedy. The chart is breaking the downward trend. Buy, buy, buy. All so important, once upon a time.

Sam sits up in his simple metal frame bed, picks back up the paperback book, and fingers through it to the place where he had left off. He gives up after just a few paragraphs. He has read this book before, and it wasn't a very good book to begin with. Sam has never been a bookish man, he has always preferred movies and television. A teacher in school had once called him a visual learner. Sixteen books sit in a neat stack next to the bed. They cover every genre. Classic, mystery, fantasy, science fiction, collections of short stories, an inspiring tale of a man who could only use his left foot, and an old dog eared harlequin romance novel.

Sam lays down the book he is holding, and looks down the spines of the others, reading their titles, his eyes coming to rest on the one about the man who could only use his left foot. It is an autobiography which matches a movie Sam had watched a long time ago. Sam feels a great affinity for the man who could only use his left foot. He feels like the two of them would have understood each other. It is Sam's favorite book, except for the times when his physical needs became too strong to ignore, then the romance novel takes its place.

The books are not in good condition. Most are missing their front covers and have yellowed pages. A few even have spots of mildew spreading across sections, blurring words and plotlines, forcing Sam to fill in the blanks as best he can. All of the books are in English, which is much appreciated. He has read through all of the books at least five times. It is hard to remember exactly how many times, but he was fairly certain it is five. A few of the books are poorly written and have atrocious plots, but after the fifth reading none of them seem that bad. Sam is glad for the books, they had not been there when he first arrived.

Sam lays back on his creaky little bed and puts his head on his pillow, folded over itself to make up for the lack of stuffing. His beard and hair, long and greasy to the touch, itch. He wears a t-shirt that is now yellow, and a pair of faded jeans with no shoes or socks. The bottom of Sam's feet are black with dirt. The concrete room around him is empty and boring. Four bare walls, a floor with no markings but a drain in the center, and a ceiling crossed on the far end by a single leaky pipe. A door sits in the center of the wall to his left, and a small glazed over window sits high in the wall in front of him against the ceiling. The entire room is about twelve feet square, one-hundred-and-forty-four square feet, give or take depending on how far off his estimated dimensions are.

Sam's eyes rove across the room, he squirms to get comfortable, stretching sore out of shape muscles, eliciting squeaks from the bed. When he had first arrived he had tried to do pushups and situps to help the time go by, but it made him too tired, so he had stopped. To his left is a table and chair. A paper plate sits on the table, holding the remains of his last meal of rice and beans. Next to the plate is a plastic pitcher half filled with water. There is light outside the glazed window, which means the rice and beans were breakfast. He would probably receive the same for dinner, but maybe he'd be lucky and there would be the addition of tortillas and maybe an over ripened tomato. Once

Sam had gotten a pitcher of beer instead of water. The day he had heard gunshots and yelling outside his window. He had nearly pissed himself when the door opened. The beer had been delicious.

In the corner, past the foot of the bed, sits the bucket, with a few lazy flies bobbing in and out to gorge themselves on the feast that he provides them. When he had first arrived the smell from the bucket had made him sick, but he is used to it now. It has been easier since he had started pissing in the drain in the center of the floor, reserving the bucket for his other needs. The bucket is not all bad. It attracts the flies, which provide a much needed source of entertainment. Sam doubts that anybody can catch flies as well as he can. His bony arms and hands seem quicker than they once were, but perhaps in the heat the flies are just slower.

"I apologize for the inconvenience all of this is causing you. You should not be here long."

"That would be preferable."

"Indeed. Just cooperate with us and nothing bad will happen to you. I am a businessman, a professional. It is of the utmost importance that you always do as you are told. Do you understand?"

"Yes."

"Good."

Sam watches the square of light from the glazed window move slowly across the floor. The room is always cold, and Sam spends much of his time underneath his blanket. The blanket stunk when he first arrived, but now it just smells like him. The sunlight is bright and Sam yearns to feel it on his face. He longs to press his cheek against the window, to feel the heat from the outside world. It is more a general feeling than a need. He has everything he needs in the room.

Of course it is just a dream. He can no more touch his face against the glass than he can fly up into the sky which he never sees. The chain attached to his skinny ankle holds him back. It snakes down beneath the bed where it is set into the concrete. If Sam stretches out as far as he can the tips of his longest fingers can almost touch the window. If he was just a few inches taller he would be able to feel the warmth of the glass. Sam's ankle hurts where the cuff goes around it. When he first arrived the shackle had felt tight on his leg. Now it is loose. It doesn't hurt as much as his hands.

Sam closes his eyes and sees a man in new blue jeans sitting at a bar of marble. The man is plump and prosperous looking. He has well groomed hair parted on the right and his face is freshly shaven. Behind the bar are numerous shelves of glass, covered in bottles of different shapes, sizes, and colors. The constant hum of voices fills the room to the chandeliers hanging from the high arching ceiling, outdoing the piano being played by the man wearing the tuxedo in the corner. The voices belong to men in suits and well mannered women with tight skirts and low cut blouses. The bartender wears a black bowtie and a red vest. He wears a little black mustache just like all the men in this country. The bartender smiles at the man in the blue jeans, but his eyes scream obscenities at the gringo who thinks too much of himself. The man in blue jeans does not notice the eyes, only the cheerful smile. He sees only a man happy to serve.

The man in blue jeans laughs loudly at his own joke, slapping the local next to him on the shoulder, and then knocks back a shot of tequila. The local is pale with sandy hair. He has more Spanish blood than the man behind the bar. The local takes his own shot and signals the bartender for another round. The local returns the friendly back slap and laughs with the man in blue jeans. He calls the man in blue jeans mi amigo and they joke and laugh in loud voices as the world blurs around them.

The tequila they are drinking tastes better than any of the tequilas the man in blue jeans has ever had back home in the States. Its color is clear and the aroma of the agave fills his sinuses as it pools on his tongue. Another joke, another laugh, and the man and the local throw another shot back. The man in blue jeans is having a good time. The local takes a drink of water. The glass that he puts back on the bar contains more liquid than when it was lifted.

Footsteps above Sam's head. Heavy booted feet move across the ceiling, growing louder and then fading in the distance beyond the world encased within his walls. Big feet, heavy footsteps, one of the Big Men. Sam can tell the difference between all of the footsteps. The Big Men both stomp around, every footstep carrying the weight of their bulk and muscle. They sound very similar, but the one who has started to go to fat tends to walk a little heavier than the one who is still fit. The other two sound much different. They are much easier to hear and differentiate. The Boss' footsteps are lighter. The soft clip of dress shoes. The Boss moves like a dancer. The Snake's footsteps are the most recognizable. They brush against the floor. The Snake never fully lifts his feet. Sam hates the sound of the Snake's footsteps.

The square of light on the floor is about two and a half feet from center. Illuminating the tiny stream of water meandering its way across the concrete. Flowing from its source in the highlands beneath the dripping pipe to the drain in the center of the room. Little chunks of carefully placed rock line the waterway. Mighty cities and empires rising and falling with the ebb and flow of time. The Nile River in miniature. A paradise full of knowledge and wonders in the center of a desert of gray hardened stone. In his mind Sam can see that the river is full of boats. Warships, fishing craft, pleasure barges, and trading cogs. Moving upstream and downstream, unaware of the wider world around them. A civilization that has lasted a thousand years in only nine months, ruled over by the might of the pharaohs.

"I am sorry for what my employees had to do to you. It is unfortunate that you are having so much difficulty in learning the rules."

"I heard screaming last night."

"That is none of your business. Please trust that I know the best way to conduct my business."

"How much longer do I have to stay here?"

"I do not know. Do you know of anybody else we can speak to besides your wife?"

"What about the company? My father-in-law....."

"Ah yes, the older gentleman who told us to go to hell."

"My father-in-law never liked me. He always called me a rich girl's fling."

"So we can agree that he is not a likely source of the needed liquidity. Come now, surely you must have other family."

"No. I am an only child and both my parents are dead."

"You have my condolences."

"It's okay. They've been dead for some time. Please though, I have my wife. My wife loves me."

"I am sorry my friend. I do not believe your wife understands the gravity of the situation. We may need to convince her."

The light gives away the time of day. Sam has long ago given up keeping track of the individual days, they all seem to be the same, but the time of day is still important. When the light reaches even with the back of the bed the Big Men's footsteps will come down the stairs. They will open the door as they always do, wearing their matching luchador masks, blue with silver piping. Their brown eyes, brown noses, and brown lips poking out will be the only visible parts of their faces. The one going to fat will stand watch to one side, holding his submachine gun. The fit one will unlock the chain around his ankle and signal for him to pick up his bucket.

They will take him out of his room, down the hallway filled with doors. One on either end and three on either side. Sam assumes that behind the door on the end to the left are the stairs. He has never seen the door open, but the sound of the Big Men coming down always comes from that direction. The door on the other end opens to the bathroom. Sam's door is in the center, on the right hand wall when looking at the bathroom. The other doors are always closed. When Sam had first arrived there had been sounds from behind the other closed doors. Shuffling feet, creaking beds, sobbing in the night, and the occasional scream. The rooms are silent now. It has been a long time since he has heard any noises behind them.

The Big Men will take him to the end of the hall and allow him to pour the contents of his bucket into the toilet and do any business he needs to on top of it before flushing. Once there was a man who would never have been able to do his business while two large intimidating men watched him. Sam does not have this problem. He will sit on the poorly mounted toilet, rocking it back and forth on the bolts that hold it to the floor, and stare back up at the men staring at him, his face contorted in concentration.

If it is the third day he will be allowed to bathe in the shower so black with mold and mildew that you can barely see the white tile underneath. The shower will be cold and there will be no curtain. The soap will be rough and he will have to dry himself with a threadbare towel that is never washed. Sam likes the third day the best. Today is not the third day. When all is done the Big Men will take him back to his room and put back on his chain. They will bring him down his dinner and leave him for the night.

Sam does not believe the Big Men wish him any ill. They are not violent men. They have eyes like Labradors. Big, dumb, and eager to please their master. When he had first arrived, they had hit him often, but it was never in a hateful way. More in the same way a man cuffs a disobedient dog. Sam was slow to learn when he had first arrived. The two rules which got him beaten the most were not to talk unless spoken to and not to flush the toilet paper. The Big Men never talk to him, so he is expected to remain silent. They do their jobs without words, working with motions and gestures. It had been unnerving at first, but now seemed normal. Harder to break was the habit of flushing the toilet paper. The plumbing is bad and the pipes easily clog. The paper goes in a trash can next to the toilet.

Sam does not think of the Big Men as bad men. They are just simple men, doing a job to support their families. Sam does not know if they have families, but he likes to imagine that they do. In his mind they are no different than any blue collar worker, trying their best to get by. It makes dealing with them easier. Sometimes Sam even imagines that the Big Men like him. They had been the ones who gave him the books. Sam likes them, or at least the human contact they represent.

"I am sorry my friend, but it appears that your wife will need more convincing."

"No please. You already took a finger. She'll come through. I know that she'll come through. She comes from a wealthy family. You just have to give her more time."

"It has been three months since we sent the package. It is rare for these negotiations to take so long. Your wife is very stubborn. My associate thinks if we sent an ear, things might move along more quickly."

"God no. Not that. Please don't take my ear."

"Again, I am sorry my friend, but like I said, your wife is very stubborn."

"Couldn't you just send another finger? Please, anything but my ear."

"My associate could take things that would make you wish we took an ear, but I am not a barbarian, just a businessman. Do you think if we sent another finger it would convince your wife?"

"My wife loves me, but she has to get the money from her father. He's an old bastard. He never thought I was good enough for her. Please, I've done everything that you've told me to. I've been good. Please don't take my ear."

"This is a strange situation. Perhaps I am going soft. Do not cry my friend. We will do as you have asked. We will only take a finger."

"Thank you. Thank you. Thank you."

The man in blue jeans awakens with a splitting headache and can see nothing. At first he thinks he has gone blind, but soon realizes that he just has a bag over his head. His hands are held behind his back by metal cuffs. He can remember nothing to connect the night before at the hotel bar with his current whereabouts. A bench seat, the feeling of two large bodies to either side. A moving vehicle on a bumpy road, his body rocking as the car corners. All is silent but the sound of breathing and the occasional cough. The man in blue jeans wants to cry out, but he cannot, a rag is tied across his mouth. The man in blue jeans can do nothing but sit, and be scared, until nothingness reaches out and takes him once again.

Sam jerks awake to the sound of footsteps coming down the stairs. The square of sunlight sits halfway between the drain and the bed. It's too soon. It's not the right time. It's not part of the routine. Breaks in the routine are never good. Breaks in the routine suggest something bad is going to happen. There is no one else left, only him. If they are coming down the stairs they are coming for him. The stumps of his pinky fingers ache on both hands. His hands reach up and brush his ears.

For a moment the panic subsides with a sudden burst of hope. Perhaps the Big Men coming down the stairs is a good thing this time. Perhaps his ransom has finally been paid. Perhaps the Big Men are coming down to take him upstairs back out into the wider world. Thoughts that have long been repressed bubble to the surface. Sam can see himself getting on a plane back to Chicago. He can see himself riding in a taxi past the well manicured lawns of his neighborhood. He's wearing new jeans and a freshly laundered polo shirt. His face is shaved and his hair is trimmed, parted neatly on the right side. The taxi comes to a halt and he gets out, giving the driver a generous tip. Sam walks slowly up the winding sidewalk, past the freshly cut grass and the rosebush he and his wife planted together when they moved in. Sandy. Her name is Sandy. He knocks on the door and she opens it, her auburn hair up in a bun except for a few loose strands. She smiles and tears drop from her beautiful big blue eyes. He smiles too, and they embrace.

The fantasy falls away with each heavy footstep on the stairs. Sam's body begins to shake and tremble. He can see them coming. The Big Men and the Snake. The Snake with his dragging feet and green with purple piping luchador mask. The Snake with his thin lipped mouth and strangely pale eyes. They are cold eyes, uncaring eyes, the eyes of a monster. The Snake is carrying his box of knives. It's a beautiful box of oiled walnut, covered with ornate carvings in twisting designs. Inside are knives. Peeling knives, carving knives, filet knives, and cleavers. Sam can see the glint in the pale eyes, a little smile on the lipless mouth. The Snake takes his time and carefully makes his selection. Sam can feel the Big Men's strong arms holding him down. The fit one watching with a bored expression. The fat one looking away. Sam can see the look of ecstasy on the Snake's face as he begins to cut. The pain. He can feel the pain.

He can hear the whoosh of the torch being lit and the stink of burning flesh.

The footsteps reach the bottom of the stairs. Sam can recognize them by their pattern. There are three people. Two of them are the Big Men. Two are always the Big Men. The other footsteps are light and clip with their forward movement. The Boss always comes first. The Boss always comes to talk to him before the Snake begins his work. The Boss is not a bad man. He is just a businessman. Sam shakes and sweats as the footsteps move down the hall. He pulls his blanket up to his chin, a child hiding from the dark. They are just outside the door. The latch clicks and the door creaks open.

The fat one comes in first, his submachine gun held against his chest. Next comes the fit one, his hand resting on a holstered pistol. They stand together next to the door. The Boss is the last to enter. He wears slacks and a white button down shirt with the top two buttons undone, showing his brown chest and a tuft of curly black hair. A cream colored sport coat rests on his narrow shoulders. The Boss's luchador mask is red with yellow piping. His lips are plump and full, his nose sharp and pointed, his eyes are a lighter shade of brown than the Big Men's. The Boss walks into the room and looks down at Sam. He stands and studies him for a moment, his eyes taking everything in. The Boss misses nothing. His nose sniffs and Sam can see the revulsion in his eyes. The Boss is not used to the stink of the bucket.

The Boss grabs the chair and pulls it away from the table. He sits and casually crosses one leg over the other as though he is visiting an old friend. Sam slowly lowers his blanket until it's bunched around his waist. He nervously fumbles at his once white undershirt, hands failing to brush off the stains of old meals and dried blood, stains only noticed in the presence of the Boss. The Boss sits and watches Sam, waiting for him to quit fidgeting. The Boss looks at the remains of

72

Sam's breakfast on the table. He pushes the plate away from the edge. A hand snakes into the inner pocket of the sports coat and pulls out a pack of cigarettes. The Boss puts a cigarette in his mouth and he lights it. He starts to offer Sam one, then remembers that Sam doesn't smoke. Sam had told him that when he first arrived. The pack of cigarettes go back into the pocket.

"You are a conundrum my friend." The voice is deep and rich like black velvet. Only a hint of an accent showing that English is not the speaker's native tongue. "You have been with us here for nine months. You have been with us longer than anybody has been with us before. It has been too long. It is time for us to move on. In my business it is never good to stay in one place too long."

Sam licks his dry lips. He wishes that he could have a drink from the pitcher on the table, but he doesn't dare to ask. He doesn't want to waste his favors on frivolous things.

"My wife....."

"Your wife does not return our calls. We have not been able to get a hold of her in more than a month."

Sam rubs his hands together. His palms are very sweaty. He rubs them on the blanket. Sam licks his lips again. His eyes flick from the Boss to the Big Men, massive and silent, and back to the Boss. He starts to speak, but stops. His throat is very dry. The Boss watches patiently. Sam knows it is best for him to say it. Saying it will give him some control.

"I guess you'll be wanting an ear then."

The eyes behind the luchador mask give no hint of emotion, but the mouth frowns slightly. The Boss lets out a sigh, like a man forced to say something he does not want to say.

"No, your ears are safe, I doubt it would do any good. I have never had to hold an asset this long before."

"My wife....."

"I'm afraid that I must be blunt my friend. Your wife does not seem to care whether you live or you die. I am very sorry."

An image of Sandy appears in Sam's mind. He can see her sitting at the breakfast table doing her morning crossword. Her forehead creased in concentration. Her mouth silently mouthing the clues. Her long supple fingers toying with her earlobe as she thinks. The smile and flash of white teeth as she deciphers another answer. She can feel him looking at her, and she looks up and reaches out a hand to clasp his where it sits next to his coffee cup.

"My wife doesn't want me?"

"It would appear that way my friend. You have my condolences. This is a very strange situation for me."

Sam tries to feel something. He tries to be angry, he tries to feel sad, but all he feels is empty. There is nothing, just a hole. Sam's breathing is slow and relaxed.

"Yeah, me too."

The Boss sits and smokes his cigarette. His eyes seem to be full of pity. Sam's head is filled with Sandy. Images of laughing, smiling, and making love. Warm emotions and good feelings. Every happy moment marches past in an endless parade. His mind desperately searches for clues to make the world make sense.

"What is going to happen to me?"

The Boss exhales a ring of smoke and watches it float towards the ceiling. "It is time for me and my associates to relocate. We cannot take you with us. You are a failed investment I am afraid. It's time to cut our losses."

Sam knows that he should feel afraid, but he doesn't. His mind continues to whirl, unable to organize itself into a recognizable reality. The Boss puts the remains of his cigarette out on the table and leaves the butt. He gets up and turns towards the door, pauses, then turns back. The Boss steps towards Sam and extends his soft manicured hand. Sam takes the offered hand in his own and feels the Boss shake it lightly with a firm grip.

"It has been a pleasure doing business with you."

The two men stare at one another for a moment. The Boss' lips curve in a half smile that doesn't match his eyes. He breaks the clasp, turns, and walks out the door.

Sam watches him go in silence. The Big Men are silent too. The one going to fat holds his submachine gun and the fit one walks out of the room. He comes back a moment later with a brown bottle and a rag. The Big Men walk towards him and Sam sits perfectly still. He tries to think of his wife, but the images disappear into the empty void of his mind. What did he do? What did he do wrong? A part of him, a part long dormant, tells him to fight, tells him to struggle, but the thought quickly disappears as well. The fit man pours some liquid from the bottle onto the rag and pushes it against Sam's face. The rag smells sweet and antiseptic. Sam begins to feel woozy and then the world fades to black.

Sam's head is splitting when he wakes up. His skin feels hot like he has a fever. His head spins and his tongue feels overly large inside his mouth. He sits for a while, his back against the side of a dumpster, the hot metal burning his skin through his t-shirt. He is facing up an alley towards a dead end wall covered in graffiti. The front of his shirt is badly stained and his mouth tastes like vomit. A few chickens cluck nearby, pecking along the ground for bugs. His head finally slows its spinning to the point where Sam feels comfortable standing and he gets up and walks out of the alley.

The sun is bright. So much brighter than he remembers. Its devilish rays feel hot against his pale skin and his eyes squint painfully to survey the scene around him. He stands at the edge of a town square. A tall white church with two towers sits at one end and a gurgling fountain sits in the center. It looks like something from a tourist postcard. A gringo's imagined version of a small Mexican town. People walk across the square. Some look at him from the corner of their eyes but none stop to look directly. The sunlight grows less intense and Sam walks slowly into the square until he stands next to the fountain.

The fountain is at least twelve feet across and twelve feet high. A massive circle of stone and churning water. Sam looks down into the water and sees a distorted version of himself. A hobo with a thick bushy beard and unkempt long hair. A gaunt man with sunken cheeks and deep set eyes. The man in the water is a stranger. A character in an imaginary land. The world around him can't possibly be real.

Sam looks up at the cloudless sky and then at the world around him. His gaze follows the movement of the people until finally falling on the white edifice of the church. Sam starts to laugh to himself. It starts as just a silent shaking of his chest and shoulders, but soon grows into quiet chuckles as tears stream down his eyes. His arms hold himself in a lonely embrace and feelings long forgotten burst forth from the deep pits where they've been hiding. Happiness and hope. A flood of emotions long not felt. The world around him seems so big and frightening, but he does not care.

The outburst subsides. The chuckling quiets and his body slowly stops its shaking. The tears stop flowing and dry eyes examine the world around him, taking everything in, a feast for a starving man. The gears of his brain begin to unbind and turn again. First he needs to find a police station. Then he needs to get himself a shave and a haircut. Then he will need some new clothes. Then he can see about getting on a plane and going home. The gears grind to a halt, his mind goes blank, and the final word hangs in emptiness. Home. An image of his wife, smiling and beckoning passes through his head and is gone, replaced by blue eyes rolling with impatience and disgust. Sarcastic words and haughty gazes. Harsh words and a screaming voice raging through the night. Hopes and memories tangling until there is no discerning between the two. Sam's legs fold beneath him and his back comes to rest against the fountain. He's alive. God damn it he's alive. He's made it. He's survived. Sam stares up at the church and listens to the water churning, unsure what to do.

Apprehension

Most of the offices were dark when he got into the elevator. He'd been working on a presentation and time had sped forward faster than expected. Two floors down the elevator stopped and she got in. A brief moment of eye contact, her eyes were brown, and then the two stood facing forward, quietly staring up at the red numbers sequentially dropping down. Their breathing sounded loud in the silence.

The elevator doors opened on the first floor and he politely put a hand out so it would not close and let her exit first. He pulled out his phone, checked the time, and followed her down the hall, their footsteps echoing. She had straight black hair that hung to her shoulders and wore a combination of sweater and skirt which clung to the taper from her shoulders and the rounding of her backside. He found himself staring at her bottom, entranced by its rolling motion and praying she would not look back and catch his wandering eye.

She walked out of the building and turned right in the parking lot. He did the same. As he watched her back seemed to straighten and her gait to stiffen, as though the bearings of her knees had insufficient grease. He felt nervous, a cold bead of sweat trickled down his back. He accelerated his pace and the distance began to close. Her breathing became rapid and her hand reached into her pocket, coming out with her phone. Her movement forward started to quicken to match his brisk footfalls. His own tension grew and his strides lengthened. He pulled up alongside, his body so much larger compared to hers, and rushed right past without looking back, hoping his new position seemed less of a threat.

The Rodeo Monkey

The monkey was dressed like a cowboy. Chaps, vest, and a little hat tied onto his head with a piece of string. He rode a border collie with a specially fitted saddle, a young exuberant dog especially trained not to mind the extra load on its back. The clowns sent the monkey and his dog into the arena between events. The duo had a number of tricks. The dog would herd a group of goats back into a pin or jump over a series of straw bales. The monkey would hang grimly on to the dog's back, occasionally raking his miniature spurs to get it to go faster. Sometimes the monkey would pull out a little pop gun which he would shoot into the air or at targets held by the clowns who would fall in mock agony with every hit.

Dusty loved the monkey. Every time the monkey would charge out on his canine steed Dusty would give out a little eight year old squeal of delight and tug frantically at his mother's arm, pointing as he tried to get her attention.

"Mom. Mom. Look at the monkey."

Each time Linda would smile and hold her son close, pressing her cheek to his for a moment, and watch the running dog with the monkey on his back. Dusty would clap and cheer and the world would fill with so much happiness that for a moment Linda would feel herself be carried away to the unbridled enthusiasm of her own childhood. But such times were fleeting. The monkey would ride back out of the arena and the next event would begin. Dusty would quiet down and watch, bored by the non-monkey related competitions.

Linda didn't watch the rodeo. She stared down at the beer garden and tried to discern the shape of her husband amongst the convulsing sea of western shirts and cowboy hats. The sweaty heat of the afternoon had given way to the chill of evening. Linda had hoped that the drop in temperature would be enough to force her husband back to the grandstands, at least to get his coat, but there was no such luck. Dave was a man impervious to climate, especially while imbibing. Dave had left them and escaped into his sanctuary as soon as they had arrived in the early afternoon. He preferred the company of drunks and fools to that of his own son and wife.

Linda thought she saw him for a second, but the man was too thin, his shirt the only thing he had in common with Dave. She looked at her son, intently watching the last round of calf roping, breaking only for an occasional yawn or to pop a candy in his mouth. She could see Dave in her head, laughing and buying drinks for anyone who would claim to be his friend. Spending money they couldn't afford to spend. Once Linda had been part of that world, and had reveled in it. Now it seemed like those memories belonged to a different woman.

Linda wanted to go home. She had wanted to go home hours ago, but Dave was not so easily roused from his enjoyment. During the second round of barrel racing she had gone down to the beer garden fence and tried to spy her husband through the drunken mass. She would have gone in herself to find him, but the man at the gate wouldn't let her take Dusty in. She didn't like the idea of leaving Dusty outside by himself. It would take a while to extract Dave when she found him. Instead she had bought Dusty a hot dog and taken him back to their seats.

The last round of calf roping would soon be over. It would be followed by the final round of bull riding. Then the rodeo would be over. Linda both looked forward to and dreaded the rodeo's end. Dave would come and find them at least half an hour after the end of the last event, and then only because the beer garden would be closed. He'd come up the grandstand steps, cheerful and laughing, at least until Linda would tell it was time to go home instead of migrating to the nearest bar. His wishes denied, Dave would either respond by becoming angry and verbose, or sullen and pouty. Either way there would be a string of backhanded insults coming her way. Worse would be when they got home and Dusty got put to bed. Then would come the groping, the pleading for his marital rights, until she either gave in or he passed out. At times it seemed easier to just leave him behind. Go home without him. She had done it several times before, but all it had accomplished was a weekend sized dent in their finances instead of just one day.

"Mom. Mom. It's the monkey again. He's in a parade."

The calf roping had come to an end. The monkey rode out leisurely on his dog. Sitting high in the saddle and pumping his little fist in the air. Behind him came a parade of clowns on tiny wagons pulled by teams of miniature horses. One large boxy wagon seemed to get stuck in the middle of the arena and the clowns all gathered around to feign pushing and pulling in an attempt to free it. Fed up, one clown kicked at the wagon with all his exaggerated might. The moment his oversized boot connected with the garishly painted side, fireworks burst from the top upward into the air, exploding with thunderous booms and bright flashes of color above the arena. The crowd hooted and hollered and Dusty covered his ears.

The dog did not like the fireworks. At the first thunderous boom it ran at full speed towards the arena fence, desperate to escape, the monkey holding on for dear life. The dog jumped through a space between two boards. The monkey tried to crouch lower in his saddle, but the gap was too narrow. The monkey's head kicked back as it hit the top board and he fell from his mount at the edge of the arena. Several clowns were running towards the monkey. Dusty was standing on top of his seat.

"Mom? Mom? What's wrong with the monkey? Is the monkey going to be all right? Mom? Mom?"

Linda grabbed Dusty and held him close, turning his face away from the chaos in the arena below. The clowns clustered around the fallen rider. One took off his colorful vest and put it over the body to hide it from view. Linda felt the wetness of her son's tears on her cheek. Dusty tried to wiggle around so that he could see again. Linda picked Dusty up and started carrying him down the grandstand steps. Out of the arena. Past the beer garden. Out of the rodeo grounds. Out to the field, once grass, now dust, filled with rows of cars, pickups, and horse trailers. Linda carried Dusty all the way to their pickup. She unlocked the doors, buckled him in, and then got into the driver's seat. She put the key in the ignition.

The engine of the pickup stayed silent. Linda let her hand drop to her lap. She couldn't leave Dave. Leaving him was more trouble than it was worth. Linda realized she had left Dave's coat in the stands. For a moment she thought about going back to get it, but didn't. She sat and stared out at the bright lights of the distant arena where the announcer was declaring it was time to start the final round of bull riding. Compared to the voice over the loudspeakers, Dusty's voice sounded small and quiet.

"Is the monkey dead Mom?"

A hundred motherly answers went through her head, but not one reached her mouth. "Yeah, Dusty. I'm sorry. The monkey's dead."

Dusty started crying, big tears flowing down his cheeks. Linda leaned over and hugged him tightly to her chest. His little hands squeezed her as hard as he could.

"It's okay baby. It's going to be okay."

"But the monkey's dead." The little voice was choked with emotion.

Linda didn't know what to say. Her brain felt like it had frozen, but when she opened her mouth the words flowed out like water. "No honey, don't cry, it's okay. He was a bad monkey."

Dusty lifted his head and stared at her with puffy red eyes. "He was a bad monkey?"

"Yeah, he was a bad monkey." It felt like someone else was saying the words. "He robbed the rodeo payroll."

"Really?"

"He did. He was a bad monkey. He was always spending all his money on booze and getting drunk." Linda wanted to stop the flow of the words, but she couldn't seem to hold them back. It was as though she was just a spectator. They flooded over the banks in an unstoppable torrent. "He only cared about himself. He never gave a damn about his monkey family, he never spent any time with his monkey kids, and he was a verbally abusive ass to his monkey wife. He was a real bastard."

Silence filled the cab and Linda wished she could suck back in the words. Dusty sat looking thoughtful, taking deep breaths and snorting the snot back up his nose. His scrunched up face was a mirror image of his father's.

"If he was that bad it's probably a good thing he's dead then, huh?"

Linda took a couple deep breaths and gazed down at her son with unfocused eyes. "Yeah, I guess so."

Dusty nodded and pulled away from her. He wiped his nose on the back of his hand and pulled a candy from his pocket. The pair sat in the pickup and stared out at the bright lights of the arena, waiting for Dave to show up so they could go home. After a while Linda turned on the engine so they could listen to the radio.

Return of The Snarky Scientist

Hey, have I told you about the new diet I'm on? It's real cutting edge. I'm completely cutting out carbs; or maybe its protein, or meat, or gluten, or fat, or god I can't remember. Let me check the book I bought that tells me all about it. It has a lot of large complicated words and phrases which I don't really understand, but it sounds really scientific and has citations and everything, so you know it has to be true.

What do you mean the key to a healthy lifestyle is a balanced diet and exercise? Hell with that. This new special diet I'm on is guaranteed to prevent me from ever getting heart disease; or maybe it's Alzheimer's, or maybe it will cure my gastro-intestinal problems, or maybe the gout. It's hard to keep them all straight, but trust me, reading it will definitely change your life. Besides, all of your balanced diet and exercise bull crap sounds like it's going to take a lot of time and energy. Why would I bother doing that when I can just cut one thing out of my diet and cure everything that has ever, or will ever, ail me?

What do you mean the stuff I'm saying isn't supported by "mainstream" science? Maybe you just need to open your mind and realize that western science and medicine is killing you. People in Asia definitely don't die from the same causes as we do. Have you been to Korea, pretty much everything they eat prevents cancer. What do you mean cancer is the leading cause of death in Korea? Way to have a closed mind. After all, who in their right mind would trust one of these so-called scientists. Everything they do is highly suspect. Those bastards are probably quietly doing their research with little fanfare in their non-profit research institutions for nefarious reasons even as we speak. I bet it has something to do with the big food industry. I'm not really sure how, but it makes sense to me so it has to be true.

The author of my book, who has a doctorate by the way, would never do a thing like that. He just wants to show us a better way. What reason would he have to manipulate his research and mislead the public? It most definitely has nothing to do with the fact that he's making millions off a bestselling book and that books that say there is no easy answer and that you're probably going to die rarely sell well. I'm sure he's not the kind of person who would say something controversial to try and gain the instant gratification that only media attention and millions of people hanging on your every word can create. What's that? What about science groupies? I might give you that one, but otherwise he seems like a standup guy. Totally not the type who would play on the public's fears of illness and death for personal profit. Only asshole corporations do things like that.

Anyways, I can't stick around here talking to you forever. I have to go buy some supplements that are antioxidant, probiotic, and neutral on neurons. Yes, the author of my book is an advocate of these supplements. No, I don't see any kind of connection. Damn I hate those pharmaceutical companies who are pushing modern snake oil on dumb people who think every solution to their problems can be found in a pill. What's that? No I didn't know supplements are not regulated. I'm going to handily forget about that. No, I don't know who Harvey Kellogg is. I'm having trouble understanding what you're getting at.

Look, it's not that hard to understand. I'm just going to follow my diet exactly as the book tells me to and I'm never going to get sick, or age, or probably ever die. I don't understand what you're trying to say. What? You think rising rates of cancers and neurological disorders probably have something to do with our longer life spans thanks to science alleviating malnutrition and curing diseases that cause people to literally crap themselves to death? Sounds a little farfetched. Maybe you've been reading too many blogs.

I have to go. Have fun eating all your processed food. All that added salt, fat, and sugar is going to put you in an early grave. Yes, I suppose they could put some additives in processed food to help alleviate certain nutritional deficiencies. Seems like an interesting idea. Someone should really start doing that. No, I've never heard of goiters, rickets, beriberi, keratomalacia, pellagra, ariboflavinosis, scurvy, and keshon. They sound like made up words. Iodine, vitamin D, thiamin, vitamin A, niacin, riboflavin, vitamin C, and selenium? Now you're just spouting random science words. What do you mean cult members are normally college educated? What the hell does that have to with anything? I really have to go. Enjoy dying before me. You're going to feel really dumb.

Paradise Wasted

The ting of the intermittent rain upon the tin roof overhead was a distraction, though so was the sweat that had started laying claim to all of his crevasses the moment he had stepped off the plane. Never mind the fact that he was going on less than four hours of sleep and was still partially hungover. The fat Hawaiian woman behind the rental car counter explained again, but again it went over his head, so Paul just nodded to give the impression that he understood. The large woman looked at him for a moment, moved her neckless head in the approximation of a nod back, and got back to filling out the rental agreement. The computers were down. Everything was back to manual.

"Initial here, here, and here, and please sign here."

Paul took the proffered pen and followed orders like a champ. He twisted the document back around and the agent gave it a quick glance and then pushed forward a set of keys, motioning with her hand towards the rows of cars beyond the open air setup of the line of rental stalls.

"The car's in B8. Thank you."

"Mahalo."

Paul felt stupid the moment that he said it. He took the keys, grabbed the handle of his bag, hoisted his laptop case onto his shoulder, and headed off towards the waiting cars before he could see whether or not the rental agent was amused or disgusted at the haole taking ownership of her culture. It was better not to know.

The car in space B8 was not a compact. It was a jeep. Paul didn't really want a jeep. Other than driving a convertible, driving a jeep was the surest way to reveal to the population at large that you were a tourist. Tourists were always the ones targeted. Never mind the fact that the jeep's soft top was only a deterrent to either the stupid or the very ill prepared. Part of Paul wanted to go back to complain, but the impulse was overcome with the certainty that this was what his nod had been in approval of, never mind the fact that he was inherently a coward.

Seeing no way out, Paul accepted his fate and opened his suitcase behind the jeep. Half of the clothes were shorts and assorted t-shirts. The other half were khaki pants and button down shirts that were in need of a good ironing. The purpose of the trip was the conference in Honolulu, this was just a little personal side jaunt to the Big Island. The vacation clothes and his shaving kit all went into a smaller blue bag that folded up nicely and fit in one of the pockets of his suitcase. The now half empty suitcase was zipped back up and shoved into the tight space behind the back seat of the jeep. Paul hoped it wouldn't attract attention. He repeatedly peered into the soft plastic windows at different angles to see how visible it was. Feeling paranoid and stupid, Paul put the blue bag and his laptop bag into the front seat and got in.

The jeep started easily enough. Paul put her in gear and started driving towards Hilo. Getting comfortable was not easy. He needed to adjust the side mirrors but could find no automatic control. He tried to find the window openers, but the doors lacked any buttons or switches. The window controls turned out to be on the center console. Hilo was a bit of a maze for the uninitiated. The names of the highways on Paul's map did not match the street names within the city limits. The decision of which direction the various one way streets went seemed to have been chosen at random. He passed by the hostel once, but it took another ten minutes to pass by it again, and yet a third pass to realize that there was none of the promised parking. Seeing little else to do, Paul parked the Jeep on the street in an area marked two hour parking.

Paul got out, locked his vehicle, and started walking the one and a half blocks back to the hostel. Two cars down from his was an identical Jeep. This one with its soft top peeled back and its windows rolled down. A half open bag filled with clothes sat on the passenger seat. The crosswalks were also of interest. The buttons were placed at foot level instead of the normal waist height. Paul couldn't imagine why such a setup was being utilized, but after a little bit of thought, he dutifully hit the button with his foot. The lights changed, but the crosswalk signal did not. Paul crossed anyway.

The hostel had been a small, but successful, hotel in the first half of the twentieth century, and it showed. Up a long flight of steps to a lobby area now dominated by a long dining room table, a second long table with surge protectors for laptops and phones, and a large birdcage that contained a gray and yellow ball of feathers that emitted regular whistles and squawks of what Paul assumed to be displeasure, but probably was nothing at all. The bird was the second to reside in the cage, or at least that was what Paul surmised from the elaborate shrine of pictures and bird cage accessories surrounding a hand lettered sign that said, "We'll miss you Happy Pierre," on a side table.

The main room was otherwise empty, except for an old man watching movies on his laptop and a middle aged gentleman with a shaved head and mustache tuning his guitar. He gave a friendly smile of welcome, which Paul returned, though at a level significantly lower than what was offered. The man seemed to have the air of someone who would be full of friendliness until you broke some arbitrary rule of his own creation. The middle aged man had likely been at the hostel for far too long, probably since the day his last child went off to college and his wife realized that she couldn't stand the constant reminders of the existence of silver linings.

The door to the small office was closed and a sign declaring, "back in five minutes," was hanging in the glass window, but the woman inside motioned him to enter when she saw Paul trying to decide whether or not to knock. The woman was of Asian descent, and was likely good looking at some time before she crossed the threshold of her forties, still single and running a hostel.

"Can I help you?"

"Reservation for Paul LeFor."

"Of course, here you are. Just the one night?"

"Yes."

"Very good. You're in room 8."

She handed Paul the usual plethora of documents to sign and then started rummaging through a box of keys just out of sight behind the counter.

"Here is the one for the gate at the bottom of the stairs. We lock it after 10. I can't find you one for Room 8, but it's never locked anyway. Follow me, I'll show you where everything is."

Kitchen, please note that we do recycle, men's bathroom, men's shower, and finally Room 8. Four metal bunk beds packed tightly in a room, the lower bunks slightly larger than the top, all the bunks obviously occupied, except for one top bunk in the corner. Sheets and pillow neatly laid out, waiting. All but three of the other occupants were not around. An older man with a fringe of gray hair around his otherwise bald dome was constantly arranging and rearranging a blanket that he had hung from the bunk above to block his from the outside world. His movements were quick and furtive, like a hummingbird. A second middle aged man of Latin descent lay on another bottom bunk, fooling around on a laptop. His long hair was drawn back into a greasy ponytail and he wore nothing except for a skimpy red speedo. The third man was much younger, probably in his mid-twenties, playing on his phone. A bulkier guy, he would likely spend his later years waging a losing battle against his weight. All three looked as though they had been at the hostel for an extended stay.

The hummingbird was too distracted to notice Paul's entrance, and the out of shape Latin lover didn't seem to care. The younger guy put down his phone long enough to run his hands through a messy beard, the same thick curly red as his hair, sit up, and reach forward to shake Paul's hand.

"Chris."

"Paul."

"Welcome. Always good to know who's who. That's Mike laying down and Gary over there."

Mike didn't bother with a second glance, but Gary rushed over to give Paul's hand a couple of quick pumps before going back to his blanket. Chris was left as the official welcome wagon.

"Staying long?"

"No, just one night, then moving on to Kona."

Chris and Paul stared at each other for a moment. Neither sure what to say, until Chris broke the silence.

"Sounds nice."

With that, Chris flopped back into his previous prone position, and went back to playing with his phone. Paul glanced at his three roommates, feeling uncomfortable. None seemed like the kind that he'd want to spend much time around.

"Well, I better go get some lunch, been a bit since I've eaten."

Chris nodded, but did not look up.

"You'll find no shortage of places to eat around here."

The town of Hilo looked run down. Anything made of metal was rusty, and moss grew in every crack and cranny. Everything looked tired, still suffering a hangover from the wild abandon of its boom years, back when it was a destination rather than a starting point. Only a few white puffy clouds floated in the sky, and despite the light ocean breeze, Paul soon found himself soaked in sweat. He'd forgotten about the humidity. He had known it well the summer he had spent on Maui nine years before. It came and hugged him in the tight embrace of an old acquaintance. The type where one thought they were best friends, and the other only put up with them because they knew some of the same people.

Paul walked down one street and then another. It was an hour and a half past noon. Many of the cafes and restaurants had already closed their doors to rest and prepare for the dinner crowd. A bar was open, the three locals within watched him walk by. It was still too early in the trip to collapse down to eating bar food. A small hole in the wall joint called Paradise Burrito caught Paul's eye with a sign promising a mahi mahi burrito special. Paul walked inside. It looked as good as any other place.

The proprietor was dirty and looked like he spent his breaks smoking meth out by the dumpster. He took his sweet ass time making the burrito. As Paul waited, he listened to the only other two people in the joint, two men, one young and one old, talking about the theories of life. The young one droned on and on in a self-satisfied masturbation of his ideal. The old one interjected with softly spoken points and comments, trying to politely knock down the young one's house of cards. The young one did not notice. The burrito was much bigger than

expected. Paul took it to one of the tables outside to eat in
silence, entertaining himself by watching the weather beaten
locals and the sunburnt tourists walk by.

The burrito was spicier than expected. Paul could feel
the first hints of the heartburn he knew was coming on. Nothing
to be done. Paul walked back to the hostel. He went to the jeep
and pulled his bags out and carried them up the stairs to the
room. The hummingbird was gone, but the other two were
sitting in the exact same positions as when he had left
earlier. He put the bag of clothes and the bag with the laptop
down on his upper bunk, turned, and headed back outside. Up a
block and a half, into the jeep, and out towards the open
road. Paul didn't get far. The thought of his laptop out in the
open bothered him. He tried to ignore the thought, but it kept
nagging at him. He was only a mile out of town. Besides, he
had forgotten to grab his camera. Sighing in frustration, Paul
turned around and drove back into Hilo.

Paul drove to a garden supply store he had seen when he
had been walking to find lunch. The maze of one way streets
and guessing which was the right block only caused mild
frustration. It took asking three different people in the store, but
he left with a cheap padlock that had been hidden away behind a
display for lawn tractors. The girl behind the counter was
attractive. Dark skin, big eyes, thick hair, and curves in all the
right places. She seemed nice. Paul tried flirting a bit, but it
only made him feel old. She would be grossly obese in fifteen
years.

Paul drove back to the hostel, parking in the same place
as when he left, and climbed up the stairs again. The two
roommates were still in their exact same positions. Paul found
an empty locker on the wall by the door and put his laptop bag in
it after taking out his camera. He put the lock on the locker and
the key on the jeep's keychain. He walked back down the stairs
and the block and a half back out to the jeep. The hummingbird

was just getting into the matching jeep with the canopy removed. The hummingbird smiled and gave a friendly wave.

"Hey, look at that, same vehicle."

Paul smiled back weakly.

"Hey, yeah, look at that."

The hummingbird drove away and Paul got into his own jeep and headed back out of town. It was a nice countryside, the green in sharp contrast to the dark blue of the ocean and the light blue of the sky. Trees, ferns, and other plant life were in abundance, nearly to the point of being suffocating. It all seemed so crowded. A sign pointed towards a scenic drive, so Paul took it. He stopped here and there to take some pictures, but none of them seemed that good. When he had been up in the plane flying in, he had taken some wonderful pictures of the sun rising through the clouds. He had been so excited when he had taken them. Looking back through the camera, they seemed diminished in their grandeur. The road wound on, and Paul drove in silence, his head filled with thoughts of the past and future, few of them positive. He turned on the radio to distract himself.

The jeep moved off the scenic drive and then up a twisting road, following signs directing it to Akaka Falls. At the end of the road Paul parked the jeep and paid a man five dollars for the privilege. He walked down the trail and came in sight of the flow of water plunging four hundred feet to the pool far below. It was a breathtaking sight. The viewpoint was filled with tourists, most from foreign lands, all snapping pictures. Paul took a few of his own, but felt silly doing it. Thousands of people had all taken the same picture. What was the point of adding his name to the list?

Paul was the only one at the viewpoint not there with family, friends, or a significant other. He was the only one alone. He could feel people's eyes on him. Probing and prying. Wondering what would lead a man in his mid-thirties to be in such a predicament. Paul walked up the trail, got back into the relative safety of the jeep, and drove away. The gears of his mind were whirring, flashing pictures from his past. For a moment his mind stopped its frantic narrative and he thought about the lovely woman from the party the night before he left. She had been tall with long dark hair, and eyes that were neither brown nor green. He had talked to her for only a moment, yet she stuck in his mind. A drunk at the party had prattled endlessly on about her, much to her chagrin. It had been as though god himself had rolled out the red carpet and yelled out for Paul to look at this one. She had been the first woman in a long time that Paul had found interesting beyond the parts that would fulfill his own selfish physical needs, a short distraction from a mind that never seemed to shut up or settle down. Paul had said little to her, choosing instead to walk away. He doubted he would ever see her again.

The jeep traced its way back to Hilo and Paul found a spot half a block closer. Back upstairs in the room the pair remained frozen as though statues. Unmoved from the positions that he had left them in several hours before. Paul changed into his running clothes, not caring if either roommate saw anything. Neither seemed to notice his presence. It seemed strange to travel to such a place just to sit the whole day in bed and to never bother even to look outside. It seemed such a waste to do such a thing in such a place. To do something that could have been done anywhere. To waste so much time doing nothing. Paul stretched at the bottom of the stairs, and then went out on a jog around the bay.

It was cooler now, and the wind off the bay felt good. Paul had to run across the highway to get to the thin layer of grass between it and the bay. The bay was dirty. The water brackish and black. Men sat next to poles wedged upward in the rocks, waiting for bites. The grass widened out and he ran past long boats stored under sheds and then hotels in various states of decline. Paul's knee hurt so he switched between running and walking. It would be dark soon. Paul turned back and followed the same course in reverse. On the way back he stopped at the grocery store and bought an apple and can of juice for dinner.

When he got back to the hostel the pair were still in their places. Paul ate his dinner and took a shower. He sat in the main room and did work on his laptop, watching the various denizens of the hostel come up the stairs one by one. A few couples. A few young. But most old and alone. Even the young ones looked a little lost. Like they were looking for something that for some reason they thought might be in Hawaii. Paul sat, worked, and tried to force himself to stay awake until at least ten. If he stayed up until ten the jet lag would be easier. Memories floated in his head of nine years ago in Maui. The hostel in Paia. The nights drinking and dancing. The friends that he had never seen again. So many good memories.

The clock struck ten. The hostel owner came out and covered the bird cage. The goal had been met. Paul locked back away his laptop. The phone kid was rolled over and asleep. The Latin was still typing away in his speedo. Both had wasted their entire day. Several people were already asleep in their beds, but the lights were still on. No one had bothered to turn them off. Paul turned off the lights and climbed into bed.

Arzuw

The five men on their five donkeys rode across the stream and up the bank. The donkeys were so short that the men's feet drug through the water. Jeyhun the father, Ruslan the son, Nepes with the laughter in his eyes, Azat the nodder, and Erkin the quiet one. The father and son were clean shaven, but the rest sported pointed beards. The donkeys moved without directions from the men. They had made this trip many times before.

"Is it true what they said in the village," asked Ruslan, "is my Uncle Eziz finally coming home?"

"Of course it's true," replied Nepes, "Arkadag has released all the politicals."

"It is true," added Azat, "we heard it from the man on the radio."

The three bearded men smiled and Ruslan smiled with them, but his father's face stayed stern.

"The man on the radio is just a mouth. He says what he is told."

Azat and Erkin stopped smiling, but Nepes just grinned the wider.

"Come my friend, why must you be so dour? Why can't you smile on the day your brother comes home? It has been long since we have seen him."

"I shall be happy when I see him."

"You should be happy now. Eziz is coming home and things have changed."

"I do not see how things have changed."

"You should grow back your beard like us. You used to have the most magnificent beard in the village."

The other two men nodded in agreement.

"I'm going to grow my beard out," piped in Ruslan, "as soon as I am out of my father's house, and it will be the most magnificent beard in the village."

The men laughed and Azat clapped Ruslan on the back. Jeyhun let out a sigh.

"What my son does when he is out of my house is his business, but until then he will stay shaven. Eziz had a magnificent beard as well once, just another thing he refused to compromise."

Nepes let out another laugh. "My friend, Turkmenbashi is dead, and all his crazy ideas with him. Things are going to change."

"So you say," replied Jeyhun, "just as they changed when Turkmenbashi kicked out the Soviets."

"The Soviets were much worse than Turkmenbashi," stated Ruslan.

The four men looked at him. "How would you know," asked Jeyhun?

"That is what they say in school."

"School is good," replied Nepes, "but they should teach facts and not opinions." The other three men nodded.

The men rode in silence and the dry grass of the hills gave way to the green of cotton fields. Farmers, stooped to work, rose and watched them as they passed.

"Things are going to be better in Turkmenistan," said Nepes. "Eziz coming home is proof of that."

"It is true," agreed Azat.

"I do not see how things being better for Turkmenistan will be better for me," replied Jeyhun.

"It will be better for us too," answered Nepes.

"Under the Soviets I was a herdsman. Under Turkmenbashi I was a herdsman. Now it is Arkadag, and I am still a herdsman."

The men rode in silence.

"How will things be better," asked Ruslan?

"We won't have to obey silly laws anymore," replied Nepes. "We will have more freedoms than before.

"We will have electricity in the village," said Azat. "We will no longer have to buy batteries for the radio."

"We will all have fine horses instead of donkeys," stated Erkin. "Just like the ones on the national emblem."

"We will have all that and more," said Nepes. "Eziz is coming home and things are getting better."

The train appeared in the distance, stopped at Ali's warehouse just outside of the town. Men worked loading and unloading crates, watched over by a man holding an AK-47. Ali owned the market in the town, and all that came on the train was his. It was a short train, only six box cars and a caboose. It only made the trip to town once per month, to bring what Ali sold, and take away what Ali bought. One of the boxcars was painted bright blue.

"Look at that boxcar," said Nepes. "Have you ever seen a boxcar painted like that before?"

"No," replied Azat, "never have I seen a boxcar painted like that. It is a sign, a sign of change. Eziz is coming home and things are already changing."

"It is just a blue boxcar," stated Jeyhun.

The men rode down by the train. Ruslan's body shook with excitement and the others looked about them curiously, waiting for Eziz to appear. Men kept moving crates, and the man with the AK-47 eyed them warily. Erkin rode up to the locomotive and started talking with the engineer. After a few minutes he rode back with a couple packs of Russian cigarettes he had bartered for. He calmly sat on his donkey and lit one, exhaling smoke from his nose.

Nepes broke the silence. "Well?"

Erkin shifted himself on his donkey and offered each of the men a cigarette in turn. Nepes and Azat took one, but Jeyhun and Ruslan did not. Erkin lit the cigarettes for them and sat in silence until his was done.

"There is nobody on the train."

The men all looked disappointed.

"He must have missed this train," said Nepes. "These things take time. Eziz will be on the one next month, and we will come down to meet him."

The other men nodded and kicked their donkeys to get them moving back towards home. The three bearded men joked and laughed, while Jeyhun and Ruslan fell behind.

"Father," asked Ruslan?

"Yes," replied Jeyhun.

"If Uncle Eziz had been on the train, how would he get home? We only have five donkeys."

Jeyhun said nothing and kicked his donkey to catch up with the others. Ruslan looked back behind him, at the train with its blue boxcar, and thought of all the changes that would happen when his Uncle Eziz came home.

Misidentified

Wally brushed the sweat off of his brow and ran his fingers through the widow's peak of his retreating tightly curled hair, which was frizzed out more than normal due to the high humidity. He looked down at his white tennis shoes, stained red by the wet dirt of the small side road which cut its way through the jungle, and scraped them against a rock to knock the mud off their bottoms. He knew it was useless to do this, both ahead and behind him was more of the same red mud, but he did it anyway.

Wally's bony hand, connected to his skinny arm, scratched at his little droopy paunch belly before resetting the tuck of his bright blue t-shirt, with Panama emblazoned across the front in bright orange letters, in his khaki shorts. This was about the twelfth time he had re-tucked his shirt since leaving the Playa Blanca resort on his little hike, an act he knew was slightly neurotic, but not something he could compel himself to stop. The shirt always seemed to be working its way out of place, and even tightening his belt until it was most definitely too tight did not seem to help alleviate the problem. To make matters worse, his power walking seemed to constantly shift his shirt in one direction and his underwear in the other. However, that problem he had only had to fix twice so far.

Wally was just glad that he had forced himself to wear low cut socks, though he hated how they revealed his skinny legs and shapeless calves. If he had worn socks that reached up to mid-calf he knew he would be constantly stooping to pull them back up. His calves were hairless from the constant motion of such past endeavors. Wally preferred higher socks that reached to just below his knees. At the very least they seemed to stay up better. Wally's appearance did not give the impression that he really cared what others might think of him, but even he had to acquiesce to the fact that the combination of knee high socks and khaki shorts would have looked fairly ridiculous.

Wally took off his glasses, little round spectacles that an accountant would have found passe, and wiped them with a carefully folded bunch of toilet paper from his pocket. The rain had passed an hour ago, but like tucking in his shirt, he found himself unable to stop wiping his glasses. Earlier he had crashed through some low hanging palms and ferns, too busy staring at a busy highway of leaf cutter ants scurrying in a long line across the road to notice his surroundings. Now every time he cleaned his glasses he also checked the lenses for scratches. His wife used to call him finicky and fidgety. Granted, she had used a loving tone, at least until ex was added to her title. After that she usually referred to him as a high-strung melon headed piece of crap, and those were her kinder terms.

Wally continued forward on his walk, an excuse to avoid sitting on the beach, socializing with his friends, and watching the constantly lapping waves. These were all fine things, but enough had been enough. Besides, he imagined even his friends would eventually get tired of him complaining about the quality of the rooms, and that was all he really had to talk about. As he walked he found his hand absentmindedly checking to make sure the zipper of his fanny pack was secure. Somehow in his head he could just picture it coming open for no obvious reason and his belongings unknowingly being lost in the jungle all around him. This would be a bad thing, considering that the fanny pack held his passport, wallet, and room key. In essence, his identity.

The brand new guidebook that Wally had purchased just before the trip, the so called vacation, for $15.99 plus tax had warned him to keep these three items on himself at all times. Panama was apparently filled with thieves, at least according to the book, and Wally had no other trusted sources of information. Wally could have purchased the same book used at the same bookstore and paid half the price, but he couldn't even touch a used book without thinking of some stranger, with notably less than Wally's hygienic standards, reading it in the bathroom. The new book, while higher priced, was most likely much less handled. To be extra safe he had taken the fifth one from the front.

There was a safe in his hotel room, but Wally had chosen not to use it. The pictures of the resort from their website did not give a good representation of reality as far as Wally could see, and it gave the entire place an unreputable air which made him doubt the trustworthiness of anything they provided. He was already sure that the maids, a group of heavy set dark colored women who smoked in the stair alcoves and didn't understand a word of English, had been going through his bags when they cleaned his room. Carrying what he could with him at all times seemed the safest bet.

Never parting with his precious fanny pack did have some side benefits. Mostly in that Wally could beg off swimming in both the ocean and in the resort's pool, which it claimed was the world's largest, though Wally was sure that was a lie as well. Wally had nothing against swimming, but he loathed bathing suits. Wally did not like the sight of his pudgy droopy body with its sunken chest. He resembled a pot-bellied stove held up by two skinny sticks. Being in a bathing suit made Wally feel uncomfortable, and he doubted it did much to improve anyone else's day either.

It was peaceful and quiet on the little side road, not a single sound, except for the constant buzz of insects and the chatter of the birds. Granted it was hot and humid as hell, but it seemed a worthwhile trade off in place of forced small talk and polite comments about the weather. Wally could almost feel like he was enjoying himself when his precious solitude was broken by rhythmic squelching sounds that came from around a bend up ahead, the road hidden by the thick jungle to either side.

Wally stopped to listen. The noise grew louder. A white horse trotted into view. The horse was bow backed and scrawny with its ribs poking through its hide. The bottom half of all four legs were stained red and each hoof made a slurping sound as it was pulled upward from the muddy surface of the road. On the horse sat a small man riding bareback, wearing old faded blue jeans filled with holes and a light cotton shirt unbuttoned to his navel. On his head the man wore a floppy straw hat with the front of the brim turned up in the Panamanian style. In his hand was a large naked machete, spotted with rust. The horseman pulled back on his reins next to Wally and gave a curt little nod of his head.

"Hola senor."

Wally didn't really know much Spanish and he really didn't want to be bothered, but it seemed rude to not acknowledge the obvious greeting.

"Hola," he returned.

The man smiled, showing crooked yellow teeth beneath his black mustache.

"Muy bien tiempo que estamos teniendo hoy."

Wally couldn't even guess at what the man had just said. He recognized the word good, but that was about it. He wished the man would get his horse out of the way so Wally could continue on his walk, but the man wasn't moving and his words seemed to require some kind of answer of affirmation.

"Si," said Wally.

The man's face shifted into a look of quizzical curiosity and he spoke again, gesturing back and forth with his machete.

"No suelo ver a muchos turistas en esta carretera. Te has perdido?"

The man gave a little laugh. Wally wasn't sure what to say. He thought he recognized the word tourist, but he couldn't be sure. The movements of the machete were making him nervous and his eyes kept darting back and forth between the man's dark face and the dull metal of the blade. The man seemed to be expecting him to say something back. Not knowing what else to do he stretched his face into the most congenial smile he could muster.

The man smiled back, showing his yellow teeth again, and for a little bit they both stared at each other, smiling and feeling uncomfortable. The two men's eyes roved up and down each other's bodies, sizing each other up and taking notes of every detail. Wally noticed how the man's gaze fell upon his fanny pack, moved on, and came back to it several times. The way the man eyed the fanny pack made Wally nervous and he felt sweat trickling down his spine. Wally suddenly became very aware of how far away from the resort he actually was and warnings from his guidebook began to float through his head. The man leaned forward and gestured at Wally's fanny pack with his machete.

"Esa es una muy buena canguro mi amigo."

Wally felt his body stiffen. He looked furtively behind himself and then behind the man with the machete leering down at him from his horse. Wally recognized the word friend, but the rest to him was just a jumbled mess. Wally found himself wishing he was back amongst his friends, and not on some lonely side road in the jungle. He pointed down at his fanny pack with a single shaking finger and his voice sounded strained in his ears.

"Canguro?"

"Si, canguro. Estaba pensando en la compra de la misma por mi esposa. Le importaria que le eche un vistazo a la suya?"

Wally did not understand a single word this time, though the word estaba sounded uncomfortably like stab to him. In his head, Wally could see the man slashing at him and laughing like a deranged maniac. Verbal understanding wasn't really necessary. As the man spoke he gestured with the machete again. The gesture seemed to imply, hand over the fanny pack gringo before I make you bleed. Wally could feel both his legs trembling in fear. He didn't really see what other option he had. There was no one else around, jungle on both sides, and the man had a horse and a machete. There seemed to be no safe options besides obeying.

Wally reached down and with shaking hands slowly unbuckled his fanny pack and stepped forward to hand it to the man on the horse. The man took it smiling and Wally took a few steps back. The man held the fanny pack up, his eyes roving across it as though he was examining the fine stitching and the quality of the zipper and buckle. The man muttered to himself.

"Bueno. Bueno. Un muy bueno canguro."

The man was distracted. Wally saw his chance. The man had what he wanted, but who was to say he still wouldn't kill. Wally turned and on quaking legs ran as fast as he could back up the road, fueled by adrenaline and terror. Wally could hear the man yelling behind him and then the sound of the horse being kicked into a trot.

"A donde vas!? Tu olvidado tu canguro!"

Wally could hear the horse getting closer. He could hear its heavy breathing as it closed in. Wally saw in his mind's eye the man's face grinning like a lunatic as he raised the machete and brought it down into Wally's head, splitting it as easily as a melon. Wally didn't want to die. Wally wanted to talk with his friends again. Wally wanted to swim in the ocean. Wally wanted to live. Wally gave a feral scream and threw himself off of the side of the road into the jungle, ripping his way through the fronds and ferns where the horse hopefully could not follow. A branch ripped the glasses off of Wally's face, but he did not slow down. He was like a deer hunted by a wolf, desperately flinging itself forward to escape. Behind him he could hear the man on the horse still on the road, yelling at his retreating back.

"Que estas haciendo!? Estas loco!? Olvidaste tu canguro! Olvidaste tu canguro!"

An Accident

The big Cadillac hit a bump and the cassette tape dropped from Larry's ten year old fingers as he tried to shove it into the stereo. The tape clattered as it fell out of reach onto the floor next to Grandpa's feet. Grandpa looked at Larry and smiled his little warm smile. The smile which said not to worry, it was no big deal. Grandpa ducked his head and reached down to find the tape. Larry watched Grandpa as he lifted a half used package of gum, took a quick glance out the windshield, and then resumed his search. Larry looked up at the trees and buildings slowly sliding past, and then looked back down to help. In his head Larry could already hear the music on the tape. The old country songs that Grandpa loved.

The crash was more of a bump. A sudden deceleration from twenty to zero. A quick halt due to the American Motors Hornet in front of them stopping to obey the red sign on the side of the road. Larry felt his body pushed forward into his seatbelt. Grandpa banged his head against the open ashtray and came up cursing softly. He rubbed the side of his head and looked at Larry, his eyes full of concern.

"Are you all right?"

Larry nodded.

"Okay. You stay here."

Grandpa undid his safety belt and stepped out of the car. Larry watched him as he walked to the front of the big Cadillac and bent over to inspect the damage. The driver of the other car did not get out. Larry could see the back of the man's head, wisps of silvery hair. The other driver seemed to be angry. The man's arm rose and fell, slamming his hand against the dash. Grandpa straightened up, smiled at Larry, and gave him a thumbs up. Larry returned the gesture.

Grandpa walked to the other driver's open window and leaned over. Larry saw Grandpa's smile turn into a frown and his eyes change from cheerful to angry. Grandpa reached into the Hornet and grabbed the other driver by the shirt front. His other hand closed into a fist and punched the man in the face. The driver struggled but Grandpa held on, his fist and arm moving back and forth like a piston, the driver's head rocking back with each blow.

It only lasted a few seconds. Four quick punches. Grandpa let go of the man's shirt. The man's head lolled loosely on his shoulders. Grandpa walked back to the Cadillac and got in. He was breathing heavily. He reached down and picked up the dropped cassette and handed it to Larry without comment. He put the big Cadillac in gear and pulled around the Hornet. As they drove by the other car Larry could see the driver, an old man, crying, and trying to stifle the flow of blood from his nose.

Larry turned around and stared at the man next to him. Larry's eyes were as wide as saucers and his mouth hung open loosely. The elderly man beside him was a stranger. Grandpa was a sweet carefree man. Larry had rarely seen him mad. Grandpa was the type to steal your nose and slip you a piece of candy with a sly wink when your Mom said no. Grandpa was the type that sat on the floor with you to play with the plastic cowboys and Indians. The type that read your favorite stories before you went to bed. There had never been any evidence before that beneath that kind exterior beat the heart of a psychopath. If he was willing to accost a random motorist, god only knew what else he was capable of.

Grandpa took his cigar out of the ash tray. He did not relight it, but sat staring straight ahead, gnawing at it, his jaw clenched. Larry sat perfectly still. Staring up at the man he had thought he knew so well. It did not seem prudent to ask questions. Grandpa ran one hand through his thin gray hair and spoke without turning his head away from the road.

"You going to play that tape or just hold it all day?"

Larry looked dumbly at the cassette in his hand. He reached forward and pushed the tape into the stereo. The drawl of Hank Williams filled the Cadillac's interior. Grandpa turned and looked at Larry and saw the look on Larry's face. Grandpa smiled and gave Larry's leg a shake, but his eyes still looked angry. Larry kept quiet, wary of the deranged maniac sitting next to him. Larry tried to stare out at the road, but kept looking at the old man out of the corner of his eye.

Grandpa looked at Larry again.

"You all right?"

Larry nodded.

"How about after we get some gas we go get some ice cream? Does that sound good?"

Larry nodded again.

The big Cadillac turned into the gas station and Mark, the gas attendant, jogged out smiling and waving in his white uniform. Mark's usual lines, almost out of his mouth, were swallowed when he looked into the interior of the car. Mark looked at Grandpa, then at Larry, then at Grandpa once again.

"Jesus Lou, you look like hell. Everything okay?"

Grandpa nodded his head. "Yeah, everything is fine. Just got into a little fender bender."

"Christ what happened? Everybody all right?"

"Yeah, everybody is okay. Just hit the guy ahead of me at a stop sign. No real damage."

"Well that stinks. Was the other guy mad?"

"No, not really. When I walked up to his window he had his dentures out, whacking them against the dashboard to knock some of the teeth out."

"Really? What the hell?"

"Yeah, what a son of a bitch."

Transition

"I want to give it three more weeks."

He knew where that came from. He wished that he hadn't asked the question the night before. At the time it had seemed for the best. He was tired. They had reached an impasse, both just repeating what they had said before. Talking more would add nothing. They both needed time to mull it over. It had been part of a series of rebuttals, a question answering her statement. She wanted more time. How much time would that be? It was meant as a question without an answer, a point of how things would not change. She had seen it differently.

He sat in the tub, filled full with hot water and epsom salts to ease the pain in his leg. The epsom salts had been her suggestion. The soreness of the leg was a constant problem made worse by a decision to commute into work that day on his bike. The first time in a long while. He sat and stared down at his genitals floating in the water, modesty between the two of them seemed pointless, studying them as he tried to put his thoughts in order. She sat on the lid of the toilet, turned to face him, legs crossed, leaning forward just enough to provide a hinted view of the top of her small bust under layers of tank top and half unbuttoned sweater. It was not seduction or enticement, just a woman long used to dressing as she did.

He looked up at her face. It was a child's face, a little chipmunk staring down at him with mouth slightly open. It was a child's face on a woman's body. With a woman's needs and a woman's memories, but none of it showed in her face. Her face was soft and rounded, and her brown eyes big and bright, unshaded by the cynicism and pain that clouded his own. Looking at her it was hard not to see her as a child, though their ages were close to the same. When they went to bars together she was always carded, while with him they never bothered. It wasn't fair to look at her in such a way, and he knew that it changed his judgment. He sat in the tub with his tired face, etched by pains and sorrows, and saw her face and assumed she knew little of either. She had pains and sorrows, most of which she had told him, but yet the child's face remained, only marked by a few solitary strands of silver winding their way through her black hair.

The pitter patter of small feet on the hardwood. Her small dog came around the corner, a mutt of chihuahua and jack russell lineage, tongue lolling and eyes bright like those of its master. The dog had been a stray once, wandering the street, searching for scraps, desperate for love. She had fallen in love with it from the first moment that she saw it. A kindred spirit. He reached out his hand and the dog took a few steps forward into the bathroom, and then retreated back to the doorway, worried that it was bath time for it as well. The dog looked at him, waiting for something to happen, hoping that when it did it would not be bad. He noted how she had the same look upon her face.

"What would three more weeks change?"

"I don't know. I just want to try for another three weeks."

118

He paused and looked away again. Three weeks did not seem so bad. After all, he had originally planned to say nothing for an additional two weeks. Her life had been so shitty of late, between work and volunteering, a maelstrom of her own creation. For her it was better to brace, lean, and push forward, rather than speak up against the weight. He had not meant to bring it up in the movie theater the night before. It had slipped. She could see that something was wrong and it had escaped before a white lie could be formed. She had started crying, and they had left before the movie started, her hiding her face from the curious onlookers, him holding his bag of half eaten candy.

The idea of three weeks was enticing. Perhaps it would be easier in three weeks. No, it would not be right. He knew that he would not feel any different in three weeks. He knew he would feel the same. He would be giving her hope where there was none. Besides, he doubted that he could handle breaking her heart again. This was the fourth time, and he doubted a fifth would lighten the burden.

The dog, growing bored by the lack of action, turned and walked back out of sight around the corner. The two of them sat and listened to the sounds of the dog playing by itself with a tennis ball in the other room. The hard bounce of the ball against the hardwood punctuated the silence. At times the ball rolled into view and the dog came scrambling after it, both of their eyes following the dog, before it disappeared once again.

"I don't think it will change anything."

"Can't you try? Can't you try it for me? I never ask for anything."

It was true. She never asked for anything. In all the time that he had known her he had never seen her push for what she wanted. Never saw her provide more than a token resistance to his own demands. When she offered up ideas he did them, as long as he had nothing else better to do. When he offered up ideas she did them, always making the time whenever possible, just glad to be spending time by his side. It was not that he never did anything exclusively for her. It just took more effort to get himself to do it. He did owe her. The balance of accounts were most definitely in her favor, and he was not so self-absorbed to fail to see it. But it didn't change the facts, and he knew giving her what she wanted would make nothing better beyond the present time.

"Why do you want this so bad? What is it about the idea of this?"

She was silent for a moment, and the dog's bark echoed across the house as it yapped at something outside the front windows. Maybe a bike, maybe a bird, maybe nothing at all. It was hard to guess with the dog. Last week it had been eating flies it caught mid air. He had laughed and she had looked on with pride.

"Quiet!" Then back to him. "I don't know how to explain it. I feel something about this, something that I haven't felt before. I feel like there's something here. Something worth fighting for. I don't know how to describe it."

He knew that she did know how to describe it. He knew that she could describe it with a single word but wouldn't. That word had certain risks, and she would not risk pushing his slow retreat into a hurried flight by using it. He felt for her. What she was feeling was not a mystery to him. He had felt such things himself. He knew the risk of having a stronger need than the one towards which you are pulled. He did not want to hurt her like he had been hurt. He wanted to treat her better than the way he had been treated.

"I just don't feel the same way you do. I care about you very much, but I don't feel the same way."

The small dog came around the corner once again, shaking at the sight of the tub. He rubbed his fingers together and whistled, smiling gently as she sat quietly. Slowly the dog moved forward, furtively step by step. Backing off, but then moving farther forward than before. Finally coming into reach, he brushed his fingers along its fur, the former stray arching its back before scurrying away. Both of them smiled at the dog's retreating back. The dog was good. The dog would help her through the pain as it had done before. He wanted to be careful in all of this. She had come into his social circle alone, abandoned by friends of her last failed relationship, and he did not want to drive her from all that she had reclaimed.

"You're one of the nicest people I've ever met."

"I don't need you to tell me I'm a nice person."

That wasn't how he meant it. She was one of the nicest people he had ever met. There was not a sour or bitter bone in her entire body, and much of her time was spent thinking of others. Of all the women he had dated, none had ever treated him better than her. She listened when he needed to talk and was patient at all the right times. When she listened he could tell that she truly listened, and she never forgot anything that he told her. She was his biggest promoter, investing time into his dreams, and would let nobody speak badly of him, even himself, even when the words were not untrue. When he was down or hurting she would do her best to cheer him up, even buying him little gifts from time to time. All that he had ever bought her was a bottle of lube.

It wasn't that he did nothing. He too listened to her problems, let her vent when it was needed, and found little ways to cheer her up when she was feeling down. But it wasn't the same as it was for her. She did them because of how she felt, and he did them because it felt like it was owed. He was glad when she was happy, for he did care about her deeply, but the investment was not the same. To him it felt like she worshipped him, which left him feeling uncomfortable. He often wondered if she saw the bad along with all the good.

"Can't you try? Please try."

Her eyes were sad and desperate, and he could not look at them for long. The tub was growing cold and the hour was growing late.

"I'm going to get out of the bath."

"Can we keep talking?"

"Yes."

He pulled the plug and the water began to gurgle down, once full of endorphin inducing heat, now just cold and uncomfortable. He stood and dried himself with a towel. He could not help but notice her eyes tracking the body that only a few days before had been pressed up against hers. In his mind he could see the curves of her own supple body. Softened by the giving of all of herself to him, but still hard from the marathons which had helped distract her from her last loss. He could feel stray sparks snapping in his brain, flashes of their coupling and her giving in to his perversions, though in fairness, over time she had enjoyed them as well. It was how they had started, nearly a year ago, just two people aiding each other in taking care of a bodily need. In that at least he had never felt like he had cheated her, always giving more than he took.

He slipped on his robe and swept the thoughts away, blowing out the sparks before they caught and ignited into a wilder fire. Such things must be in the past, sacrificed to the flames of his own righteousness. They sat on his bed and didn't say a word. The dog came in, prancing, with the tennis ball in its mouth. They took turns throwing the ball, ricocheting it off the wall into the front room. The dog each time leaped down off the bed and gave chase, scrambling on the hardwood, unable to gain good purchase. Both of them smiled and the dog seemed to smile too.

"She's not afraid to jump up on the bed anymore."

In his head he could see an image of the little head, poking above the mattress edge, whining because it was too scared to make the jump. It had taken some time, but the fears had disappeared, and the dog thought nothing of it now.

"Yeah."

"I wish you would try."

"I don't think it will make a difference. I don't think I'm going to feel any different after three weeks."

"How do you know unless you try?"

"It's just how I feel."

"Are you sure you're not just afraid? You said yourself that this was farther than you normally go. How long has your longest relationship been? What, two months?"

"Three months."

"You see. You yourself said that you have problems with committing. Problems with anxiety."

Part of him wished he had never told her about those things, the scars of past loves. It had been good to get them out. Good to say them out loud. Being with her had forced him to take a light into the dark crevasses where such things hid. Clean up all the junk that was holding him down. He had always had doubts. There were doubts when it had been just sex, there had been doubts when they tried actually dating for the first time, and there had been doubts when they had started dating again a month ago. That had always been the question. How much were the doubts how he truly felt and how much were they just creations of his own mind. There was only one way to find out. That is why he had come back. Anxiety could only be beaten by going after it head on. Forcing yourself to survive it. It was not an enemy to be beaten by logic or happy thoughts. It must be beaten by action. She was a wonderful woman, and they did work together well. He had to be sure. He had to conquer his dragons, and that meant bringing her along for the ride. At least she had been forewarned. He did that part right.

"I'm not going to deny that I have my problems, but I don't think they're the reason why."

"How do you know?"

"I just do."

"But can't you try? Why can't you try?"

"I have been trying. What do you think I've been doing for the past month?"

They had talked many times about his doubts in the last month, but he had never told her about the worst of it. He had never told her how much the little things affected him. Introducing her to his friends, bringing her to social events, telling people they were dating. He never told her about the uncontrollable shaking, the thoughts careening out of control through his mind, the desperation, and the wondering if he was going insane. His primal brain would scream out in panic, ringing every alarm to warn of danger that wasn't there. This was not a new feeling, it was not as frightening as it had once been. He knew that they meant nothing. He just had to ride them out to the end. He didn't tell her about the fits of madness. He didn't want her to worry, and he didn't want her to hang on by using his problems as an excuse. He had been in that place himself before, and he knew the damage that such thoughts could cause.

"I know that you've been trying. I just want you to try more."

"I know how I feel. What is going to happen after three weeks have passed and things are still how they are? How are things going to be different then?"

"I don't know. I don't think you can say for certain either."

"Would it be easier for you to let go then compared to now?"

"I don't know. Maybe."

"It's not as though things will be different. I've known you for a year now."

"Yes, but the stuff we were doing when we first met was different. We weren't dating then."

"What about the first time we tried it."

"Things were different then. You yourself said you weren't trying as hard as you could. That you had a lot of problems."

"I don't see how things are going to be any different."

"I don't know either. That's why we should find out."

"What good would it do?"

"At the least things would be less stressful for me. I'd have less shit going on. Couldn't you do it for me? Couldn't you lie to me until things are easier."

"I'm not going to lie to you."

"God damn it, why not?"

"I'm not going to lie to you, it wouldn't be the right thing to do."

"That's easy for you to say. This is easy for you."

It was easier for him, that was fair, he was the one who got to make the decision, but it wasn't easy. He wanted to love her. He wanted desperately to feel what she felt. He enjoyed being with her. He enjoyed hanging out. He enjoyed so much about her. Here was a woman who was fun to be around, who had been shown all his flaws, who loved him unconditionally, and whose only want was to be with him, and he couldn't love her. That had always been the crux of the issue. There was so much of his shit in the way. She had waited patiently while he cleared it out. But no matter how much shit he got rid of, no matter how much he forced himself to conquer his own fears and problems, the doubts were always there, just as strong as ever. Until finally they could be ignored no longer, and he knew just how he felt. Mentally, he had not been in a better place for the past three years. He was emerging stronger than before, and the cost was her broken heart.

If he didn't care about her this would be easier. He could walk away and never look back. He could turn the corner and pretend that she was fine and not crying by herself. It would be simple. He wouldn't have to give it another thought. But he did care about her. He didn't want her crying by herself. He didn't want her all alone. Perhaps it would have been better if he had just walked away, but it was too late now. He had never wanted to hurt her, and had avoided doing so as much as possible, making the present situation worse.

"When we started this again we discussed that this might happen. You said you knew the risks."

She said nothing. The dog hopped back up on the bed, the only one still smiling. It turned over on its back and she rubbed the little animal's belly, staring at her caressing hands. She looked like a sad lost child and he wanted to gather her in his arms, hold her tight, and tell her everything was going to be all right. He wanted to comfort her, tell her that he had changed his mind, and do his best to make her smile. But he didn't. He would know that he was lying to her and lying to himself. He'd be unhappy, and no matter how much he tried not to, he knew that he'd start to take it out on her. It wouldn't be fair. It wouldn't be right. It was better to do it this way. Giving her false hope would only make it worse. It was bad enough that he had come back, but he had to know for sure.

"I'm worried about this wart."

He looked down at where her finger pointed, at the growth on the dog's belly. He leaned in for a closer look and brushed it with his finger to gauge the dog's reaction.

"It doesn't seem to be bothering her. It probably isn't anything to get excited about."

"Are you sure?"

In these things she trusted his judgment. He had always been around animals. This was her first dog.

"Yeah, just tell the vet at your next regular appointment. He'll probably just freeze it right off."

Silence once again, except for the gentle scrape of the dog's slowly wagging tail brushing across the blanket and the electric hum of the refrigerator in the kitchen. He tried to think of something to say, but couldn't, at least not anything that would help the situation.

"Is there anybody else?"

"No."

The half-lie came easily, without hesitation as though it was the truth. There were no other women. There was no one to step up to take her place as soon as she was gone. He did think about other women. He thought about them all the time and at times even flirted and enjoyed it, but later felt guilty. She did not like it when he flirted with other women, but it came naturally with his every word.

"How can you be so sure?"

"Because the feeling is always there. I've never felt the same way about this as you. For a long time I blamed my problems and my anxieties, hoped that if I got rid of them I would. But no matter how much I worked on my problems, no matter how much I put behind me, how I felt didn't change. I wanted it to change, but it didn't. I felt like I was living a lie. It made me unhappy."

She burst into tears and he sat not knowing what to do as water poured down her cheeks and her body was racked by sobs. The sudden breaking of the dam scared the dog and it flipped back over to stare worriedly up at its master. He reached his hand out to her shoulder. She sat as though it wasn't there. He felt awkward so he took his hand away.

"I can't believe you said that."

"Said what?"

"You said I made you unhappy."

There it was again. The old negative he had been waiting for. The voicing of the belief that the failure of the relationship meant there was something wrong with her. That somehow she had failed. That she was not good enough as she was, and that the only reason things had not worked was because she hadn't molded herself into the correct shape to meet another's needs.

She had been through years of shitty boyfriends, many who had treated her quite badly. She had hung on desperately to each one, waiting for the moment that they would give her the love that she knew she deserved. She had always been the one rejected, always the one turned down. In her entire life she had never had it in her to stand up for herself. She was always the one giving in, always the one finding compromises, always the one to accept excuses. In her big brown eyes the world was a wonderful place, where good things always happened to good people, and any adversity could be conquered by always trying harder. If you believed hard enough, you could make your dreams come true. The people in her world were good until proven to her to be otherwise, no matter what anybody else said.

He knew the world was not like that. He knew that you could give everything you had and still end up with shit. The world was hard, and the people in it were complicated. He knew you had to watch out for yourself, stand up to make sure no one took advantage of you. He knew that even good people would take advantage of you, walk all over you if you let them. He had been through the school of hard knocks, and the purity of his childhood views had long since been spoiled and ruined. He knew that he was as rotten as all the rest, and how easy it was to treat somebody like shit, when they never speak up in their own defense. He knew why the world kept hurting her, and that it would continue to do so until she cast aside her veil.

When they had started again he had hoped if the time came again, it would be her making the break, not him. Him doing it was just another in a long line. Her doing it would be the breaking of the cycle of her being a victim. But it seemed unlikely that it would ever happen that way.

"You don't make me unhappy. I care more about you than most people. I meant the relationship made me unhappy."

"What's the difference?"

"I love being around you, but always feeling like I was living a lie made me unhappy. You're my best friend. I've told you more than anybody else. I want to still be there for you. I want to hear about your day and tell you about mine. I want to go out and have fun with you. Why is that not enough? Those are the good parts. Why do you need the rest?"

She said nothing. Her sobs continued. He sat at a loss for words, knowing that anything else he added would likely just make things worse. All he said was true. He wanted his friend. He couldn't give her the relationship that she wanted, but he felt that what he could give was better anyway. He had never had a good relationship, and he didn't put much value in them, but friendships were a different story. She sat and sniffed quietly. The dog crawled into her lap and she petted it without thinking.

"I just wish you would try a little longer."

"It wouldn't change anything."

"How do you know?"

"I just know."

Impasse. They had reached a point of impasse once again. Just like the night before. They had made progress, but they had collapsed into reciting their positions, and no further advances would be made that night. Things had to be given time to settle.

"It's late. We both have work in the morning and I think we both need time to think about everything. Is it okay if we go to bed and talk about this more tomorrow evening?"

She nodded her head and the two rose and got undressed. Her clothes fell around her, leaving just her tank top and bottoms for the sake of modesty. It was how she had always slept, at least until his hands in their passion tore the last coverings asunder. His eyes followed her curves and he felt the hunger again, but he ignored it as he knew he must. He went to the bathroom to brush his teeth and by the time he came back in she was already laying beneath the covers, the dog sitting by her side. Her eyes looked sad and desperate, staring at the wall in front of them. She was slipping under. He cursed himself for a coward, for he knew that he should push her down. It would be quicker and probably better. But he had done it to her several times before, and he didn't know if had it in him to do it to her once again.

He was being selfish. He knew what he needed to tell her. He knew that he had to make her understand that it was her not standing up for herself that made her so unattractive. People want somebody who cares about them, but not to the point where they feel like they're taking advantage. Even the worst person will start to feel guilt if they're always given their way, if the victim of their wrongs just takes everything they give without a word of protest. We don't live in a world of childhood dreams, we live in a hard world of harsh realities. He had to tell her. He owed it to her. Even if it meant her getting hurt and mad, even if it meant her never speaking to him again. She would be better for it.

He took off his clothes, standing naked in the light, turned off the switch, and crawled into bed. It's how he had always slept, so it made little sense to change it now. They sat silent in the dark, him looking up at the ceiling, and her lying on her side and looking at him.

"What time do you have to get up tomorrow?"

"I need to be at work by 7. So probably about 6:15."

"Okay."

"It's funny to think about."

"What?"

"A few days ago I was going to let you put it in my butt tonight."

He could remember the conversation. The two of them embroiled in their passions. Her asking what he wanted. Him answering as he always did. Her resisting. Sometimes she would relent. Other times she would postpone it until a later night. He was always gentle, and did his best to make sure it was pleasurable for her, and barring that, at least not uncomfortable. If she was to be believed, she claimed that she enjoyed it.

"Yep."

It was a useless gambit. A desperate foray by a desperate woman. Such reminders of what she offered would do little. He already knew and was mourning their loss, the acceptance of his perversions being low on the list of everything he'd miss.

The dog burrowed beneath the covers between them to escape the cool night air. It curled into a little ball between their bodies, taking up a greater space than its small body would suggest. He lay completely still, not wanting to disturb the dog. One foot hung out the end of the blankets, and one shoulder enjoyed the sheet but nothing more. The rest was taken by the woman and the dog, but he said nothing. He could imagine her in the darkness. Her eyes closing as her tired brain slowed, still desperately searching for ideas to save this thing she wanted so desperately.

He had to tell her tomorrow. He couldn't let it go on anymore. He was being selfish by not doing so. Taking the easier path for himself. It would hurt her, forcing her to see, but she would be the better for it. She would miss the world that she currently lived in, just as he missed his time there as well. He could still remember how it felt, but it had to be done.

"Thank you for always being nice to my dog."

"What?"

"You know, always letting her sleep in the bed and always being kind to her."

He smiled in the darkness. She said it like it was a surprising thing to do. The dog was important to her, and she was important to him, so he treated the dog well.

"What else would I do? I guess I could put her in the attic but then we'd constantly hear her little feet moving around up there all night."

"You don't have an attic."

"I do. There's a hatch in the hallway."

"How do you get up to it?"

"I bring in the ladder from the garage."

"What about before people had ladders?"

"People have always had ladders."

"No, before they use to use beanstalks."

There was something in her voice that struck him right to the core. A lilt of whimsy that made him imagine the woman next to him as a small child. Smiling up at the world with wonderment and innocence. Bad things had happened in her life, but still her spirit was not tattered. It did not carry the scars that everyone else did. It was still fresh and new. Every part of him wanted to reach over and hold her and protect her. He wanted to shield her from the all the wrongs of the world. So many people once they had lost it, tried to go back, faking it as best they could, but in her it was still unspoiled, a thing of beauty and magic.

In his mind he could see her sticking her tongue out with a mischievous look in her eye, as she had often done before, reveling in the sunlight of a world untainted. For her, all of it was still so beautiful. How could he take such a thing from her? How could he take from her the thing he wished most for himself? He was a cynical bastard with a mind aged past his years. Yes, she would be better off seeing the world for what it was, but it would cost her something of great value. It was an orchid in a garden of weeds. It was something worth protecting. Something worth saving. He knew it could not last forever, but he would be damned if he would be the one to destroy it.

Her breathing grew regular and she drifted off to sleep. He lay in the darkness, feeling the breathing of her and the dog next to him. Tomorrow would be another day, and another evening of slowly weaning her from her need for him. There was nothing more to be done tonight. He closed his eyes, and waited for sleep to come.

The Environmentalist

In our cities we live under a dome of light. A protective blanket of ambient photons which blots out the heavens so that only the strongest stars poke through. Protected by our luminous dome we are allowed to grow big. We are allowed to see ourselves as giants, centers of our personal universes. We grow beyond our limits, held back only by the gravity of our own problems which seem to increase in scope even as we do. Our heads brush the sky, but our spirits are crushed inside. Giants have giant problems.

I grew up where you can walk in places where no one else has stepped in at least a year. A place where views unmarred by the creations of people can still be seen. I grew up on the edge of the world, where the dome of the light is gone, and one is forced to look upward each night and face their insignificance. Before the majesty of the distant suns and the arch of the Milky Way we are nothing compared to the vast void hanging over our heads. Compared to the night time sky, we are less than ants.

Is it any wonder that people have so long hidden themselves from the night? Our ancient ancestors huddled around their campfires, reassuring each other in hushed voices that soon the light of day would come, blocking the universe from view. We fear it, but we crave it too. The night sky makes us nothing, but it makes our problems nothing too. The blackness is a comfort to a troubled mind, for the problems of ants are nothing, and something so small can be easily overcome.

When I was a boy people came to the edge of the wild and asked to build cabins along the creek. They offered money for the comfort of feeling small. The people were turned away, their attempt to buy the right refused. The money could have been taken, but the cost would have been far too high. If the cabins had been built, if the people had been allowed to come, they would have wrapped their arms too tightly, and smothered the wild in their loving embrace.

For these urban people the edge of the wild is not a home, but a church. A sanctuary for the relics of a forgotten life perceived to be more simple. A place where they can gaze upwards into the face of god, or the vastness of the universe, and have the problems of their lives be humbled, and brought back down to proper size. When they return to their dome of light, they will soar to greater heights, their chains momentarily broken.

The giants will stride amongst the hills, and more will come and follow. Pilgrims on a holy trail of redemption. Their multitude of feet will scar the land so they'll build paths with rules not to stray. The road to self-actualization and worship will be set. Treading off the path will become a sin, and everything off of it will become sacred. Every blade of grass and every single tree will gain significance and become holy.

The world will change, as it always does, but on the edge of the wild the change will fill the big people with fear. To their eyes, the changes will seem sudden and harsh, an illusion created by the breaks in time between their pilgrimages. The creek will shift, the trees will fall, and the hills will slide until they are flat. The big people will not allow such a despoiling of their church. They'll come with money, they'll come with tools, they'll bring their big ideas. They'll seek to preserve what is always changing. Based on memories bloated to the unreality of an idealist's perfection.

The world will become made of glass, too delicate to touch. Human endeavor will become a cancer and banished from the land. Those who call the edge of the wild home will be sent away, replaced by caretakers who will strive to keep it all frozen in its place in time. The wild will become a garden. Tamed and wrapped in chains. People will still come to the sacred sight, but the power will be gone. They'll sit in cabins, eating s'mores, and wonder why they come. No one will wander the hills, no one will look up at the night sky, and no one will remember how it felt to be small.

Baby

We were all sitting at the dinner table the first time Baby brought up that she wanted to get the gastric bypass surgery. Momma was dead set against it from the beginning. I can still hear Momma's high pitch voice squealing across the room, her hands frantically smoothing the tablecloth.

"Oh god no Baby. You don't want to do that Baby. You'll die on that table Baby. I just know you'll die."

Baby just stared down at her marshmallowy hands, biting her lower lip, her face scrunched up that way it would get when she was upset.

"But Momma….."

"Oh no Baby. Please Baby. You'll die on that table. Lord I just know you would just die."

It was always pointless to argue with Momma when she got herself worked up into one of her fits. No damn use at all. Baby shut her trap and Momma went back to eating her chicken. Baby didn't go back to eating. She pushed her bucket away and tears started flowing down her face. Momma didn't notice. She kept her eyes on the table. I waited until I knew Baby wasn't going to eat anymore, then finished her chicken up for her. There was no food wasted in that house. Momma's house. Momma's rules.

Baby was always fat. Hell, even her baby pictures looked fat. When I came along she was already ten, but chunky enough that she mostly wore sweatpants to school. Things did not improve as she got older. Baby just got bigger. By the end of high school her going to the doctor for knee and joint pain was a regular thing. She couldn't cut it in college. Too much walking around to class. Baby was back home before the end of the first year. When she got back Momma just hugged her tight, told her there there, everything will be just fine, and brought out a big old chocolate cake she baked special for the occasion. That cake didn't last too long.

Baby never really knew her daddy. Momma always said he was a big man. A big man with a big appetite and a laugh like a train whistle. Baby always said I was the lucky one. Lucky because I had the skinny daddy. Gave me my skinny genes so I could eat whatever I wanted. Baby always blamed her daddy for giving her the wrong genes, making her fat. I don't know. No one would ever describe me as skinny. I never met my daddy either. Momma just always called him the skinny one, but then again, Momma had never been a small gal herself.

By the time she hit twenty-five, Baby weighed four hundred pounds. She had to go on permanent disability. Hell of a thing to see. A woman her age, having to wheel around town in one of them scooters. Use to drive me nuts when I was in high school. Sitting there, trying to watch TV, listening to Baby wheezing.

"Choo choo," I'd say, "coming down the number four track, the express to Atlanta."

Baby would get mad. Who could blame her? I was being a little shit, but what could she do about it? She was stuck there on the couch. Down there on the far side where no one else would ever sit because it was all caved in. She'd just scream and yell until it wore her out, then go back to wheezing again. God she had a mouth on her. If Momma was about she'd give me a smack. Yell at me to leave my damn sister alone. Never really fazed me much. Seemed like about anything got me a smack back then. I guess at the time I didn't feel too bad for Baby. It seemed like she was in a mess of her own creation.

In all fairness, Momma certainly didn't help the situation any. When Baby's daddy cut loose, he left Baby and Momma in quite a bind, or at least that's the way Momma put it. Lots of living out of cars and doing the best you can type of stuff. There were a couple of years there where things were pretty lean, though you wouldn't have guessed it looking at the pictures of Baby. Either way, when Momma got the good job down at the courthouse, she seemed to make it her mission in life to make sure her kids never went hungry again. We never had much for Christmas presents, but lord, our house was always full of food. Momma liked watching us kids eat. I'm betting it was her favorite thing in the whole damn world.

That first time wasn't the last time that Baby brought up the surgery. For a while it seemed like there was a big fight about it every month. Every time it ended the same way. Momma getting all hysterical, spouting no Baby this and no Baby that. It didn't take long until it was just the two of them screaming at each other. I'll give Baby props. She did her research. Read up on it as much as she could. Knew all the ins and outs. Figured out all the risks. Hell, even called the insurance to make sure they would cover it. It didn't matter. Anytime Momma even got a hint that Baby was looking into it she'd freak out, screaming and crying.

"Don't do it Baby. God sakes, please don't do it. They'd kill you on that surgery table Baby. Kill you straight dead. Then where would I be Baby? Where would I be?"

There was just no reasoning with her. I stayed out of it. You know how Momma gets. There ain't nothing you can do when Momma gets that way.

I think what really got Baby starting to think about getting the surgery was after she got stuck in the tub. Momma and I were both at work. She was taking a shower and slipped, fell right on her back and couldn't budge an inch. Spent a good hour in there screaming before anybody heard her. Finally Mr. Johnson next door found her and called the fire department. They called Momma and me. It was quite an ordeal to get her out. I didn't go in. I didn't want to see Baby that way. Besides, there was nothing I could do that the firemen weren't already doing. Momma was convinced they were going to have to bust up the tub. She spent the whole time fretting, making plans for what we'd do for showers and the such until we could get it fixed.

They got Baby out just fine, nothing hurt but her pride, but she was real quiet for the next couple of days. Then one night at dinner tears started flowing down her face and she just started balling to beat all. Momma of course came all unglued. Peppering Baby with questions to try to figure out what was wrong.

"What's wrong Baby? Why you crying? Tell Momma honey. Tell Momma what's wrong."

Baby had to choke out the words. She couldn't get herself to stop sobbing.

"When the firemen were getting me out of the tub. One of them...."

"Yes Baby, yes, what did the fireman do?"

"One of them put his hand in my vagina."

Momma just came uncorked at that one. Started screaming and pounding the table. I thought the damn vein on her head was going to pop. She just kept yelling, more noise than words.

"Those bastards. I'm going to kill those bastards. Don't worry Baby. Momma's going to get us a lawyer. Momma's going to make sure those bastards rot in hell."

Baby kept crying, but started freaking out too, waving her arms around, trying to talk louder than Momma."

"No Momma. It was an accident Momma. An accident. He didn't mean to do it. He just couldn't tell one fold from another. It was an accident Momma."

You could see the gears shift in Momma's head. I'm willing to bet without a clutch.

"Christ child. An accident. Why'd you freak me out like that? Are you trying to give me a heart attack?"

Baby stared down at her dinner plate, her face bright red. Momma just kept right on a going.

"Don't I have enough stress without you adding to it? Good god what a shock. Christ Baby, if it was just an accident, why are you balling?"

Baby just started crying again. I felt like I oughta reach over and give her shoulder a squeeze or something, but I didn't. I just kept eating. I didn't really want to get involved.

"You just don't understand Momma. You just don't understand."

Momma and Baby fought about that damn surgery for a little over a year, right up until the day Baby died. It was during that real hot weather in July. Baby went out to the store to get a soda. The batteries on her scooter went dead halfway back. She decided to try and walk it. Died right there on the sidewalk. Heart attack at thirty-one. Hell of a thing. Just a hell of a thing. We had to get a special wide casket so we could bury her. Momma was inconsolable. She just kept screaming about Baby this and Baby that. Blubbering to beat all. I don't know. Just a hell of a thing. It was about three months later that Momma got that gastric bypass surgery. Slimmed her right up.

Delayed

The solid smack of the deer against the front of the pickup put an immediate end to the fight between the kids that Nancy had been futilely trying to end. The attention of everyone was suddenly shifted to the brown body and stick-like legs flying forward and the sudden pressure against their seat belts as Nancy brought the pickup to a sudden halt. When all momentum ceased, Nancy sat back in her seat and let her breathing fall back to normal. She looked at the two wide eyed faces next to her.

"Is everybody okay?"

The two blonde heads nodded in unison and then leaned forward to try and see the mangled body of the deer, which was thankfully hidden from view by the hood of the pickup, except for two hind legs feebly kicking next to the right front tire. Nancy took a few more deep breaths.

"You two stay in. No funny business."

Without waiting for a reply Nancy opened the door and got out. She walked to the front of the pickup and looked down at the deer. She turned her back to the scene and gazed across the empty windswept ridgeline. The highway was an empty black ribbon stretching as far as she could see. Her eyes followed the line of a barbed wire fence until they fell upon a rock crib. She walked off the road towards it.

The kids waited in the car as they had been told to do and watched the deer's feet kick, telling each other dirty jokes that mostly consisted of the shock value of using curse words to pass the time. Both felt sympathy for the deer, but the emotion was small compared to the worry that the accident would extend the half hour drive home to the point that they would miss the start of their favorite show. The fact that their mother would now have no patience for the rest of the evening was also of concern.

The kids watched Nancy walk back to the highway, carrying a rock the size of her head, cradling it in her arms as though it was a bag of groceries. The rock was obviously very heavy given how much she struggled with it. Her face was set in a neutral position and her eyes seemed to be looking at something very far away. When she got back to the front of the pickup she hefted the rock over her head and brought it down as hard as she could in one swift motion. The legs of the deer jerked. Nancy lifted the rock and hefted it over her head again. Down came the rock. The deer's legs jerked again, and then stopped moving.

Nancy stood for a moment breathing hard. She lifted up the rock again and threw it into the ditch on the passenger side of the pickup. The kids watched it roll, one side dry and one side wet. Nancy leaned over and started tugging. The two hind legs disappeared out of sight. The kids leaned towards the driver side window to try and get a better look, but their seatbelts held them back. All they could see was the deer's four legs pop into the air as Nancy rolled it into the ditch.

Nancy walked off the highway and rubbed some dirt on her hands. She walked back to the pickup and got in. The kid's eyes stared at the spray of red spots on the cuff of her jeans. She

146

took a couple of deep breaths and then turned to look at her gaping children.

"It would have been cruel to let it suffer."

Nancy put the pickup back into gear and drove off down the highway. The kids were well behaved for the rest of the trip home.

Malas Noticias De Mi Amigo

The swarm of red broke free from the swarm of yellow on the field below, pushing the ball forward out in front. The fans in the stands above, a sea of red except for a small inlet of yellow surrounded by a fence and police, rose from their seats and started screaming in a fever pitch of excitement and hope. One figure in red appeared in front of all the others, kicking the ball forward, flanked by two of his comrades on either side. A wave of thirty thousand voices washed down upon the pitch as he reared back and kicked with all his might. The big goalie in yellow threw himself to the side in an attempt to block, but his efforts were useless. The wave of sound crested and fell back. The ball flew harmlessly to the left of the net.

Fernando sat back down and took another plastic cup of Balboa beer from the short styrofoam container on the seat next to him. Taking off the beer's plastic lid he scooped some ice from a small plastic bag at his feet, put it into the cup, and took a drink. The styrofoam could hold twelve cups, but only contained four. Of the missing, Fernando had drank six, while his friend Luis, sitting in the seat on the other side of the container, had only consumed two, well behind his normal pace.

Luis had not risen with the rest, but had instead remained seated. Fernando looked at his friend from the corner of his eye. Luis had been complaining of not feeling well since they had arrived at the match. Fernando doubted that the ten quail eggs doused in thousand island dressing his friend had consumed had helped matters any. Fernando had suggested as much, but every time the man with his big glass jar had walked by, Luis had waved him over. From the look on Luis' face, things had definitely not improved.

"Are you okay my friend?"

Luis grimaced and rose from his seat.

"I'm not feeling so well. I'm going to find some food to help settle my stomach. Do you need anything while I'm up?"

"Would you mind taking a pee for me?"

The two laughed at their old long running joke as Luis pushed past and worked his way up the stadium's stairs. Fernando took another drink of his beer and went back to watching the game. The score remained tied at 0-0 with only twenty minutes left in the second half. Panama needed a win against Jamaica. A loss would not be the end of the world, but a win would help clinch them a position in the upcoming World Cup. The red and yellow moved forward and back across the field. Two armies desperately clawing for territory and control of the ball. On the edge of the field a ring of helmeted police, some with dogs, stared upward at the crowd, hands on their holstered nightsticks, riot shields leaning against their legs.

The battle raged on. Both teams seemed frantic and desperate, but neither was gaining the upper hand. The ball broke loose and a man in red sprung after it, the shooter from before, running at full tilt with the mass of other players behind him. A challenger came in from the side, the shooter's footwork moved the ball around the challenger unabated. The crowd rose as one to their feet, yelling and screaming encouragement. A defender moved to block the shooter's path, but again the dancer's steps, and again the shooter broke free.

The big goalie in yellow danced from side to side, alone and unsure which direction he needed to leap. The shooter, moving at full speed, reared back his leg, and the crowd fell silent in anticipation, their lungs filling with the expectation of a unified victorious scream. A flash of yellow from behind the shooter. A slide to block the way. The ball shot off to the side, deflected, and the shooter fell in a tumble of limbs, tripped up by the recently dodged defender, who had chased after and thrown himself in a last burst of desperation.

The referee waved his arms, signaling that the block was clean. The crowd's lungs burst in screams of anger and hatred, peppered by the occasional curse which rose above the volume of the maelstrom. Fernando heaved his beer, plastic cup and all, out over the crowd in front of him. A torrential downpour fell onto his back from those above. The police down below tensed and prepared, ready for the chaos that might soon come, but in the end their preparations were pointless. The yelling of the crowd receded, and one by one they fell back into their seats to finish watching the match.

Luis came back down the stadium stairs and squeezed by to reclaim his seat. His hands were empty and his face was red. He stared forward, but yet seemed to be not watching the match. Fernando picked up another beer, removed the lid, and dropped in a small handful of crushed ice. He offered it to his friend, but Luis waved it off without looking. Fernando smiled and took a drink.

"Did you see that shit?"

Luis answered in a flat voice.

"No, but I heard it over the speaker in the bathroom."

"Can you believe that call?"

"It was a bad call."

Fernando leaned over and gave Luis' shoulder a friendly slap.

"How did my pee go?"

"Bad news my friend, you shit your pants."

Fuck

"Hey, you got to come over and see this!"

His message delivered, Dusty runs back up the beach with a strange skipping bound that one only sees when drunkards are full of energy. I look at the other people sitting around the fire and they all mentally shrug and go back to silently staring at the flickering flames, hypnotized by the randomness, asses planted in their camp chairs. I grab another can of beer from the cooler and turn to follow Dusty. The conversation here is lacking to the point that just moments before I was seriously considering giving up for the night to put my head down in my tiny one person tent to sulk disheartenedly until sleep overcame me. Better to go out and explore than to sit here in sullen drunken silence.

The people around the fire are not bad people, or necessarily even boring people. They are just victims of a weekend of drinking and revelry. Since Friday afternoon, when they first headed out, it has been nothing but booze and constant attempts to one up each other in acts of wild youthful debauchery and detachment from reality. Now these last few survivors huddle around their fire on Saturday evening, somewhere between drunk and hungover. They have put up a good fight. They have had a good time. All wish to go to bed, but none want to be the first to break away to do so. They sit and wait for the herd to break, loathing their companions' stubborn pride.

The wild ones are all gone. Some have passed the threshold and lay in huddled heaps upon the beach along the river. Dead to the world and all the goings on around them. The craziest, the ones still fully awake, have gone off to other fires where the hooting and hollering of restive souls can still be heard. All that is left behind are those too tired to continue forward, and those who no longer have any reason to go out looking.

Each fire is a tribe, and an attempt by an outsider to enter may result in open arms and a beer, or hostility and a closed fist to the temple. It's usually better if you know a few people at a fire. Someone who can vouch for you and who can back you up when your beer soaked mouth gets a little out of hand. Going to a fire where you don't know many people greatly increases the chance of getting socked in the mouth just because some puffed chest prick doesn't like your look. Given the nature of the Riggins Rodeo, it would most likely be some loud mouth cowboy still hopped up on adrenaline and overwhelmed with the need to prove how tough they are after a poor showing at the calf roping.

My companions at the quiet fire don't even say a word as I leave. The quiet fires are different from the loud ones. You only join a quiet fire when you know people. Most of the people at a quiet fire tend to be couples, lounging next to each other, no longer feeling the need to join the peacocking of the singles at the wild fires. They are confident in their guarantee of intimacy, and look in disdain at what they consider the childish antics of their unpaired friends. Also around the quiet fires are the awkward and the shy. The introverts who have run out of gas and can no longer raise the energy to join the cacophony of the ferals dancing around their distant flames.

I am one of the latter, but at least I still have the energy to escape when the opportunity presents itself. Dusty has given me an avenue, a chance to keep this weekend from becoming a failure, and I take it. It isn't that it has been a bad weekend. On the contrary, it has been a very fun weekend. One of the best ones in a while. But to a twenty year old virgin, any weekend where one does not cure their affliction, is by all rights a failure. It's not that I am consumed by my bodily need, it's just that I think about it all the damn time.

In reality the problem is one of my own creation. An inability to focus on one person for the necessary amount of time to form the sense of intimacy needed to make such an act take place. Instead I flit about from person to person, always finding myself in the same desperate situation as the hour grows late and the party breaks up. My permanent state of being alone is set to continue for another night and I'm filled with a combination of depression and panic. Recess time is over, and I haven't even joined the game.

To make it worse, it's a problem that I'm fully aware of. It's not an issue of ignorance. The solution is obvious, but at the end of each night I find myself once again down the same well-trodden path to the same hated destination. The quiet couples all around me don't help. Living examples of how to achieve what I want. Proof that it is possible. Fuel for guilty feelings of jealousy. Coveting my neighbor's belongings and all that jazz. Sitting in a chair next to a quiet fire, stewing in my own self-loathing and pity and hating the contentment around me. Wanting just a taste of what I subconsciously deny myself. Dusty tonight is a lifeline. The last chance for a big play, a Hail Mary to get laid. I'm not looking for someone to form a deep connection with. I just want to meet someone as desperate as me.

155

I walk slowly in the direction Dusty runs, wondering which fire he is trying to lead me to. The sand gives way beneath my feet with every step, making me constantly feel slightly unbalanced, or maybe it's just the beer. It's hard to say. I'm at the peak of the drunken scale. The height of other worldliness that can only be reached by drinking copiously beyond my limits. Each sip runs the risk of being the start of me feeling sick on the slow collapse of overindulgence, but if I don't continue I risk falling back. Just getting up out of my chair has given me new life.

The flow of the nearby Salmon River is a constant background noise in the short periods of silence not filled with the music, murmuring voices, and hoots and hollers of the surrounding revelers. A few seconds of quiet which end almost as quickly as they begin. There are numerous fires all up and down the beach. Islands of warmth outdone by the brightness of Riggins down river. Stars in the limited sky, just a wedge framed by the towering hills that form the canyon walls, twinkle down. Reflections of the beach below.

Dusty doesn't go to any of the other fires. Slightly away from them, close to a sea of multi-colored tents, a large group of people crowd around something I cannot see. The crowd is yelling, cat calling, cheering, and cursing. It's a mass of humanity with every emotion possible on display. Cameras are going off almost constantly. The flashes spastically fighting a losing battle against the surrounding darkness. I reach the edge of the crowd and try to crane my neck to see over the pressed bodies. Everyone is looking down at something on the ground in the center. I tap one kid wearing a cowboy hat on the shoulder and he looks at me for a second.

"What's going on?"

My voice is swallowed by the surrounding noise and the kid turns back to try and get himself a better look. I try to push my way forward, my curiosity peaked. The loudness of the crowd is almost deafening and everyone is so tightly packed I make little headway. I stand on my tiptoes and jump to try and catch a glimpse, but no luck.

Snippets of words fly backwards out into the night. They are so jumbled together that they don't sound like human sounds. More like a herd of animals caught in some kind of over anxious fit. A big man in a baseball cap begins to push his way forward. He's over six feet tall and easily weighs 250 pounds. The crowd separates before his bulk, smaller fish parting to let the behemoth through. I slip into his wake and follow him towards the front of the crowd, the hole filling in behind us. Finally I push myself to the side and look over a stranger's shoulder at the spectacle on the sand.

It's not dark in the center of the circle. Several people hold flashlights and the constant flashing of cameras gives a unreal strobe effect to the entire scene. Like a movie's special effects imitation of a drug fueled dream. She's young looking. Pudgy in a way that softens most of her feminine curves. High school for her is not a distant memory. She is completely naked, lying on her back with a coat between her and the ground. Her legs are in the air and a weedy looking kid in a baseball cap with his pants halfway down pumps rhythmically between them. As I watch the kid gives an abrupt jerk and the crowd pulls him away and another takes his place.

There's a whole group of them around her. Most of them wear cowboy duds, but several look just like everyday college kids. The ones that have already taken their turn stand about sweating and yelling loud perverse advice at the current service provider. Their postures are straight and their chests are puffed. Proud warriors fresh from the hunt. Others stand about, rubbing their crotches and toying with their belts, waiting their turns. Some look pleased and confident, their eyes almost predatory. Some try to hide the scared looks on their faces, trying to keep themselves pumped up enough to not leave their place in line.

Most in the circle have no interest in joining the action, but are there to watch the show. Some shout out encouragement or raise their heads and howl at the moon like beasts. Others stand around, appraising the performances and making jokes, treating the spectacle as no different than the rodeo earlier during the day. Only a few have neutral faces, disguising feelings of disgust at the torrid scene. All have a hungry look in their eyes. Like wolves around a recently killed carcass, jostling and snapping at each other to gain a better view. There are several people in the crowd that I know, but I avoid looking at them. I don't want to see to which group they belong.

The crowd is too loud to hear any noise, but the girl's head is thrown back, her eyes closed, and her mouth hangs open in a silent moan. Her face is twisted in rapture and pleasure, contorted into a mask that shows no human presence. This is not a forced situation. This is a total loss of inhibition, a breaking down of all the rules and barriers of society. Tomorrow may come shame and possibly regret, but tonight all that holds us back has been swept away. For now all that are willing are welcome. For now the world has dropped away and there is only cock and cunt.

This is no tender loving moment. It is pure primeval need. All the thoughts and all the emotions stripped away until only breathing and sex remain. This is entirely primal. They seem more like animals than people, vigorously masturbating into each other. A desperate crazed attempt to escape the world using nothing but their genitals. There is no worrying about holding back, there is no caring, there is no sharing, there is no worries about what the other person thinks of the situation. This is sex boiled down to its most basic instinctiveness. A part of me feels excitement at the sight of this desperate rush against reality. A part so primitive that it doesn't even have a voice, just urges, chides me to move forward, to join the line and take my turn. It begs me to join in and forget about the world.

"Slut, you fucking filthy slut!"

It isn't until the high shrill voice bursts across the crowd that I notice the large number of women in the circle as well. They stand about on all sides. Women of all sizes and looks. They stand in groups with their eyes locked on the scene vehemently emitting hatred and disgust. A few of them look more shocked than anything else, but they are the minority. Most of the men are smiling, but all the women stare with loathing, their mouths locked in hard straight lines. They whisper to each other and point, and occasionally one raises her voice to shout out derogatory remarks. Most of the shouts are at the girl on the ground, only a rare few are thrown at the surrounding men.

The women, like the men, have collapsed backwards into more tribal and instinctual ways. Barely understood, overpowering emotions permeate the scene. A cute brunette that I had talked to earlier in the night, a good conversationalist who told me she was studying to be an anthropologist, breaks the invisible barrier around the scene, yelling obscenities. She lunges forward, screaming derivations of whore and slut, and spits on the girl on the ground. It's like a dam breaking. More women rush forward yelling at the member of their sex who has broken the rules, spitting on her in their disgust. Hate and vitriol drown out all other sounds of the night. The girl on the ground notices nothing. She is no longer a part of this world and will not have to face the consequences until she returns.

I cannot watch anymore. Beasts. I am surrounded by beasts. All the humanity has been stripped away. I push my way back out to the edge of the circle. Two girls stand nearby, their voices carrying over the mob.

"I can't believe she's doing that. What a fucking whore."

"I know, what a slut ass bitch."

"I threw her fucking clothes into the river."

"Good. Stupid slut."

My legs feel shaky and my mind is desperately trying to take in all that I have seen. I stumble off into the darkness to find the safety of my one person tent and the warmth of my sleeping bag, a refuge against the madness of the world around me. I throw the beer can in my hand away from me into the night. I desperately crave the normalcy of morning. When the beasts around me will be human once again. I want to hide. I have to escape. This is not what I want. That is not what I fucking want.

An Old Familiar Road

As the dry scablands drift by to either side his mind turns inward. For a moment his thoughts fall upon the woman. A thought that often bubbles to the top of an idle mind. Conversations never had. Dreams that never came true. Regrets that will never be fully cured. He used to fight the thoughts, pray that they would stop. Sharp pains like a sharp stick into one's eye. He does not fight them anymore. He lets them roll over him and pass back to the place from which they came. It still hurts, but it's only a dull ache now. A reminder of an old wound that will never quite heal, but can be ignored as long as one does not think about it. Sometimes it takes giving up everything you want to do the right thing. Sometimes you're the only one to know what that thing was. Memories, just memories. One mustn't concentrate on them too long. For a moment he wishes for someone to talk to, but he is alone in the car. Just him and the miles of freeway still to go.

Hank

Ellen gave her a ride to the dance, but disappeared as soon as they arrived. Ellen was on the hunt for the boy she liked. The one who used to have the mutton chops until his father paid off the barber and one was accidentally shaved. Laurel paid the two dollars to get in and went straight to the bathroom. She wanted to make sure that she looked good for Hank. In their last phone conversation he had promised to be there. She had hoped that he would ask her, come pick her up, and maybe take her to dinner first, but he hadn't. He never did. He always just met her places. He was a frugal man.

The bathroom was full of girls primping, girls smoking, and girls doing things that do not get mentioned outside the bathroom door. She quietly waited by the trash can for a place to open at the mirror, and then made her move before another could take the open place. She bent over to look in the mirror, but wished she hadn't. Nothing but flaws reflected back to her eyes. A girl going on twenty. Average in all but height. She towered over the girls on either side. She ran her hands through her long straight hair, trying to better cover her ears which stuck out too much. The other girls all had perms, curls both tight and loose. She wished that she had curls too, but her mother had told her no. As long as she lived under their roof, it would be by their rules.

She wished for many things. She wished that she was shorter. She wished her ears were smaller. She wished that she filled out the top half of her dress better. She wished that she was a secretary at some fancy law firm in the city, but that was a private wish. One that she did not mention. Her father was a modern man, and the daughters of modern men did not grow up to be secretaries. They went to college and started careers. They made their parents proud.

The bathroom door opened and Kathy Zimmerman strolled in with her slightly off gait due to her club foot. Kathy took the place at the mirror next to Laurel and started chatting with the girl on the other side. Kathy was a beauty, and she used everything she had to help people forget about her flaw. Tightly permed hair. A dress tight in all the right places. What Laurel's mother would have referred to as a little too much makeup. Earrings and necklace flashing in the bathroom lights. Laurel wished her ears were pierced. She wished she was wearing just a little more makeup. She wished that her dress, at least compared to Kathy's, did not fit like a potato sack.

Kathy was laughing with her friend, and talking about the enjoyable time she was having, dancing and laughing with some boy. The name of the boy ricocheted through Laurel's head. A quick slap to the face, waking her from her stupor. Laurel rushed out of the ladies room and craned her neck to look out across the big room of the community center. Sometimes height had its advantages. He was standing next to the punch, talking to some friends. She hurried over. He saw her and smiled and the need to rush subsided. The band started playing, he asked her to dance, and out onto the floor they went. As they twirled she saw Kathy coming out of the bathroom. The beauty gave just a glance, and then waited for someone else to sidle up next to.

He was handsome. He was witty. He was the most beautiful thing Laurel had ever seen. Bright blue eyes, thick black hair, and a matching mustache gracing his upper lip. She wished she could run her hands through his hair. He was slightly shorter than her, which made her feel uncomfortable, but he did not seem to care. One hand was wrapped in a bandage. Just a trifle he told her, an accident with a nail gun. He worked two hours away, building manufactured homes. Just a temporary position until something better came along. He was four and a half years older, a man already started in his life.

The dance ended and the crowds moved on. Ellen asked if Laurel needed a ride back home. Laurel told her no. Ellen went off to cruise the gut with her friends. Laurel followed the man on her arm out to his El Camino. Hank and his buddy Roger went into the bar for a drink. Laurel waited in the car with Roger's date. Roger's date didn't have any shoes. She had come to the dance wearing them, but had lost them sometime between then and now. Roger's date was drunk. She was at first very talkative, and then very quiet, other than a steady snore. Laurel listened to the radio. Hank had left the keys.

She let her mind wander with the songs. Soon it would be fall, and she would be going back to the city, back to university. She would be a longer ways away from Hank. When they had first met he had still lived in the city. It was before he had taken the job in Hermiston. She had met him through her brother's friend. He had asked her if she'd like to go out for a drive. She had said yes. They did it many times. One time they had stopped at a house. He had left her in the car. He had gone up to the door and knocked. A woman had opened it. They had talked a bit, both looking tense and uncomfortable. He had come back with a toaster under his arm, looking angry and sad. It had all been rather strange. One month later he took the job in Hermiston. They talked by phone at least once a week.

Hank and Roger came out of the bar. Roger collected his date and carried her to his car. Laurel scooted over and Hank got behind the wheel. He drove her the half hour to the next town over, taking her home. The drive was a silent one. Hank was a quiet man. On the edge of town Hank pulled down a gravel road a bit and stopped the car. They talked for a bit. This and that. He took her hand in his. The radio played but no one listened. He leaned over and kissed her on the mouth. He tasted like beer. He tried to move it on further, but Laurel pulled away. They sat side by side, holding hands, talking, and looking up at the stars.

Headlights turned down the road. A police car pulled alongside, its spotlight illuminating the interior of the El Camino. Sheriff Dalton had a few words with them, and then sent them on their way. Sheriff Dalton had been sheriff since Laurel was a little girl. She knew her parents would know by the time Hank got her home. They sat apart, on either side of the car, but Hank drove slowly for the last few miles. The car pulled up in front of her house. Laurel said goodbye and got out. Hank watched her walk towards the lit front door, and then drove away.

Her father was awake. He sat stiff backed in his chair, the newspaper on his lap, the television on, but only the test pattern on the screen. Laurel's father mentioned that the sheriff had called. Laurel told him nothing had happened. Her father had a few choice words, and then hunkered down into not talking to her. Laurel went to her room, her face red with embarrassment she knew she shouldn't feel. Laurel's mother lightly knocked on the door and entered. She sat on the bed next to Laurel. Her mother smelled of cigarettes. Laurel's mother talked a bit. The same message as Laurel's father, just with softer tones. Laurel was left alone. She wondered what it would have been like to do the things her parents thought she had. Laurel got ready for bed, laid her head down, and imagined herself back in Hank's arms on the dance floor.

Everyone Is Fucking With You

It is generally commonly accepted that the large corporate grocery chains (Safeway, Kroeger, Wal-Mart, etc.) don't give a rat's ass about you. If you surveyed your friends, the majority would most likely agree that these big grocery stores care about nothing except for profits and have absolutely no problem lying and spinning things to guarantee that the flow of Benjamins never stops. In such a world, thank goodness for the emergence of specialty grocery stores (Whole Foods, Yokes, New Seasons, and a myriad of others). Thank goodness there's a place to shop where you know somebody is watching out for you. Where people value more than money. Where nobody would ever blatantly lie to you or fuck you over just to make an extra buck.

Most of the chain specialty grocery stores that we know and love today really started taking off in the 1990's. The specialty grocery stores knew they couldn't compete with the big boys on price. They needed to find themselves a niche. They needed to provide a specialty product that people would be willing to pay more for. Organic fit the bill perfectly. People are only willing to pay more for something that serves the same function as a cheaper alternative if they feel like they are extracting some kind of value by doing so. Proponents claimed that organic was healthier, safer, and more environmentally sustainable. Three of the biggest buzzwords for consumers. Purchasing organic made you a better person. It as well helped feed the nostalgic need to harken back to earlier days. Times when things were simpler. Back before the so-called 'industrialization' of agriculture. You know, the time when famines and nutritional deficiency were a real thing in the United States and most people died of shitting diseases. It didn't really matter that mainstream science didn't back up any of the benefits of organic food. Marketing is about beliefs, not facts.

The marketing tactic worked amazingly well, and the specialty grocery stores saw explosive growth. While the majority of Americans continued to shop at the big grocery chains, the amount shopping at the specialty chains increased and the money rolled in. Profits kept growing bigger and bigger. More and more stores were built across the country. The big grocery chains took notice. They shifted themselves in their own slow behemoth way, looked at what the consumer was demanding, and gave it to them. They started carrying organic food at their own stores. Growth in the specialty grocery stores sputtered and profits began to sink.

The reason for this was two facets of the American consumer. The first one being that people like to do all their grocery shopping in one location. The second being that the average consumer, while very concerned about their produce, don't really give a damn about their processed food. Produce makes up only 15% of the average grocery bill. The organic produce would draw customers into the specialty stores, who would then pay the inflated prices for the organic processed goods because they didn't want to go to two grocery stores. Once the big chain stores started carrying organic produce, these consumers went back to the big chain stores. The specialty stores still had their core customers, the ones who wanted organic and natural everything, but they weren't the main source of growth in the market. Something would have to be done.

The specialty stores tried lowering the price of their organic produce to be more competitive, but this forced them to raise the prices on their organic processed foods to make up the difference, inflating the problem. The marketers then tried several new ploys to draw people back. One of the earliest was concentrating on how they treated their employees. It sold well with the people already shopping there, but did little to sway the average consumer who had to feed a family on a tightening budget. The next marketing push was the promotion of the concept of local food being better food for the environment. The idea caught hold, but again only in the area of produce. Again the average consumer didn't give a damn about processed food. Local also had the problem of it being very difficult for stores in many areas to truly source local produce. They as well faced rising competition from the growth in farmers markets. The specialty markets needed to somehow differentiate their processed foods in a way that the American consumer would care about.

Genetically modified, or GM, fit the bill perfectly. The vast majority of GM crops in food could be mostly found in processed foods, the average consumer had very limited knowledge about the subject, and the subject itself was very technical and complicated. Anti-GM activism had largely died down by this time, but a few donations to the right activist groups quickly perked it back up into fighting shape. Discussion, questions, and concerns about GM swept across the country again. Ballot initiatives started in many states aimed at requiring all GM foods be labeled.

So why labeling initiatives instead of outright bans? One of the big reasons is that outright bans are a lot less likely to pass.

Labeling can be put under the auspices of a consumer's right to know, while a ban has to go against the full weight of the scientific community. For the activists they see it as a backdoor way to scare consumers out of using GM. They hope that by putting what looks like a warning label on the majority of the food in the grocery store enough people will stop using it or get a negative belief about GM to ultimately get a ban. For the specialty grocery chains, labeling is a lot more helpful than an outright ban. The specialty grocery stores are hoping that labeling will help create their new niche market, driving people to buy non-GM processed food which they will provide, thus driving up their profits and growth.

So there you go. Everyone is fucking with you. Markets are created either by offering something better, or just creating the idea that what is being offered is better. The difference doesn't matter in marketing. But wait, many of you might say, those specialty stores are good people, they care. Well, part of that is just good marketing. The entire point of a successful marketing campaign is for you to have good feelings about the company and/or bad feelings about their competitors. So yeah, way to fall for that shit.

The Disease

You sit at the desk in the back room of your house, the one that is supposed to be a second bedroom, but that you turned into an office slash library because you live alone. Alone, the normal situation. Sitting and watching a movie online instead of going out and grasping the world by the balls. Plans and adventures always put off for another day, waiting for someone to share them with. Waiting for a time that is always in the future. This isn't a fair thing to say. You go out and socialize often. You enjoy these times alone, these times you do nothing. Yet you still begrudge yourself them, like doing them, or even enjoying them, is wrong. Like the little taste of contentment is wrong while the single piece of life is still missing.

So you sit and watch the movie, one you have watched before. The one with the guy who used to be a clown, before he started doing serious movies, and the woman who showed her cans in the movie about the ship. It's a good movie, maybe one of your favorites, which is surprising given that you have only watched it once before. Over two years ago, you watched it and cried the entire time. Memorized memories bubbling to the top. Maybe that is why it's one of your favorites, because it allows you to cry and feel.

Memories, that is all that is left, memories that should be let go of but have become an ingrained part of yourself. Good ones and bad ones all wrapped together in past failures. The dirty little secret you tell no one but yet still dominates a portion of your life. The failed attempts to reach out and try to contact the past. A past that wants nothing to do with you anymore and most likely thinks of you as a psychopath. It isn't fair and it isn't true, but that doesn't matter in the grand scheme of things, and in the end it doesn't really change things either way. A past gone from your life for three years, but still a present part of it. The sadness, anger, and regret no longer dominate your life, but you have accepted that they will always be a part of it.

It seems easier to watch the movie this time around. The scenes still elicit expected responses, but they seem more memories of past emotions than actual emotions themselves. The memories are a part of life, and though they rear their head from time to time, you know you cannot go back. Besides, it doesn't matter what you do, you know that you have done all you can, and that you cannot wait for the change that will most likely never come, and even if it did, you'll most likely never know.

You don't really watch the movie, though you sit and watch the flickering picture. In your mind it is merely background noise for an unsure brain. You hit pause and walk out to the kitchen, drink cranberry juice straight from the bottle, and walk back. The only accompaniment is the hot air from the heater, pushing back the encroaching late December cold. You pass through the living room and look at a picture on the wall. A framed picture of the moon. A yellow blob with shadows hanging in the blackness.

You took the picture, standing on your roof, playing with camera settings while imagining your neighbors thinking you some kind of nut. You took the picture, but you did not frame it. A gift, a friendly gesture, a token of esteem. In your mind's eye you can see a friend giving it to you as the two of you stand out in the cold outside her car. Conflicting emotions brought about by the token wrapped in shiny paper trimmed with a neatly tied bow. The first gift from someone who was not obligated since the past best not remembered. A simple gesture with so much more than just a framed picture you have taken hidden beneath the shiny wrapping paper.

You don't know what to say, so you just say thank you and give a hug because it feels like the obligatory thing to do. You let it go on longer than you should. You feel awkward and confused. You know this will just be more trouble, and it doesn't change a thing. Yet as you separate, get in your car, and drive away, the gears begin to churn in your mind and the doubts of your own feelings on the subject come back in, and it takes the whole next day to settle back into your earlier decision to end even the flirtation with a world that cannot be.

The first time it was easy, because you never let the illusion creep in that it could be anything but what it is. Two people practicing physical connection while closing off their minds. Throwing themselves together via the combining of their loins. Even in the beginning there were signs of where this all would lead, but verbal warnings were scoffed at and little white lies were told and you never had the guts to call her out. Instead you gave yourself the green light and said it was okay. You had done all you needed to pass the buck of responsibility and any hurt you caused could not be blamed on you.

The first time it was easy, when things finally came to a head, and all the stuff she held back finally came out. It was so easy then to move away and let it all just go, though no one really seemed to understand. For it was nothing against her or who she was, you really couldn't ask for anymore. She was kind, she was sweet, she was smart, she was deep, and good looking and dynamite in bed as well. But in it all you found her lacking, missing things for which you searched and yearned, of feelings just remembered from a past world. States of elation which had become your expectation, without which you could not see yourself in such a situation.

While you felt good about your decision, you still harbored private doubts, stemming from the past. You know that you are damaged and that demons still lurk in your subconscious. You don't know if the shakes are gone because the anxieties have been beaten or if they just slumber silently because the causation has been avoided. You want to do the right thing, you don't want to be the beast that you once long ago let yourself become. But the doubts persist, and you don't know if the decision was based upon factors that were true or false. Are your expectations reasonable, or even possibly obtainable, or are you setting yourself up to surely fail?

So your stand begins to falter and your decision you begin to question. You are lonely and you are horny, but you know that these are not a foundation you can build on. But what if this is all you can expect? You go home for Thanksgiving holiday and family comes from near and far, and all that you are missing is thrown right in your face. You know that these things are always out of reach, not by fate, but due to your own fumbling hands. But just because you can accept blame, does it mean in the current situation that you made the wrong decision? So you let yourself be carried and of your doubts you become wary, and you call up your poor friend and say you would like to give it all a try.

From the start you doubt your new decision, and you want to cry with frustration, because in your mind that missing piece must still be had. The second time is harder, four hours harder to be exact. You feel like a bastard, for within three days you have

176

risen your poor friend to the height of great elation only to smash her down as soon as she learns to fly. She begs and she cajoles, but you stand firm in your belief that this is the right thing to do. You try to explain with analogies of painting, how no matter how good one is that some just call to you without explanation. She asks questions, so many questions, and you do your best to answer, though many are of things best left behind.

It would so much easier if the past was an alcoholic or drug addict and your actions had been a last desperate attempt to see them sober once again. These are things that people can understand, unlike mental anguishes, like generalized anxieties and diseases of the mind. It just is not the same, and pretty much impossible to explain, to sacrifice your happiness to give a loved one a chance to be sane. It's all fine and good to know that you did the right thing then, but that doesn't help you move forward with your life.

Much you hold back from your friend because you don't want her to fully understand. You don't want your demons to give her secret hope. It's hard to say what's pertinent to the current situation, and hearing her own hard stories surely do not give you any help. The second time is done, and you get back in your car, feeling elated that you did the right thing in your mind. But soon the shadows of your doubts, they begin to reappear, and promises that you did the right thing sound hollow in your ears. Here is someone who loves all of you completely, and will give you anything you want so quick and sweetly, but somehow just isn't enough in your head.

Is it the right thing to do, or is it just doubt screwing it all up for you? These are the questions that run through your mind. People look for reasons, and fill the air with questions, trying to find the thing that made her wrong. But you have no real answer, just the missing piece as always, a reason you would scoff at if the situation was happening to anybody else. You sit with indecision, unsure what to do, the constant battle raging in your heart. You know it is foolish to expect the feelings of a first, but is it wrong to expect just a little bit? There are others that you think of, but they are closer to fantasy than reality, and maybe it's just a case of the grass always looking greener on the other side?

What of the damage, the broken parts inside, which you cannot deny have an influence on your soul. You can quote them all by heart, the words of the past love, that looking back gave proof to what she was.

"I want to take this slow, I don't want to have happen with you what happened to the others."

"I shake like a small dog."

"I don't know why it happens. There's no reason for it to."

"I'm fine when you are here. I enjoy being with you so much. But when you're gone, all I feel is anxiety about the two of us."

"Anxiety."

In the end it was the reason, the demon in her soul, boiled down to just a single word. You cannot help but see the similarities, between what the past tried to explain, and the very predicament you now find yourself stuck in. Perhaps it was more disease than disorder, and you have become infected, a new host with mental symptoms that hold you down. Is this a rosy apple, containing all your dreams, sitting within reach just ready to be plucked?

You see your friend a few weeks later and your doubts begin to falter, and you do things that you can't readily explain. Sure there are things missing, but so much guaranteed, and sacrifice is a known part to win the game. So you take her by the hand and lead her off again, though a part of your mind still fills with doubt. She is glad that you two will try, and you smile and half-lie, when you give an affirmative response.

The attempts at courting and relation, feels more like obligation, and you don't feel it with your heart. But you've led her off again, and you know if this is a mistake you cannot make amends, for jerking around this poor girl like you are. So you set the blame on your disease, though you know the situation is not the same, and promise to yourself you'll give it just more time. For perhaps the doubts will wash away and all the pieces will fall neatly into place.

You sit and wait to start New Years Eve, for the time to pick her up, just passing the time until then. The movie reaches its emotional climax, and you feel a single tear roll down your cheek, and wonder if you'll ever feel that way again.

The Message

Dear Dad,
Drop Dead.
Stew

Peter read the short Facebook message again. He tried to imagine his son's face contorted with rage or twisted around a sneer, but he couldn't. All the pictures Stew posted on Facebook showed him smiling and laughing. Out having beers with friends at some dive bar, a neon sign in the background. In the middle of a group of men and women wearing life jackets, packed tightly in front of a rubber raft pulled up on a riverbank. Standing behind a pretty woman with auburn hair, his hands protectively placed upon her belly. In all the pictures Stew looked happy.

Stew's eyes belonged to his mother. They looked just like Peter could remember. Peter could picture those eyes filled with fear. Fleeing from the monster. Peter wished he could go back and grab his son, take him in his arms, and tell him the monster was gone for good. Tell him that everything was better now.

Peter wished the child version of Stew he remembered smiled like the adult version did in the Facebook pictures. The child's eyes had always seemed dull and lifeless, like the person behind them was hiding from the outside world. The adult's eyes were different. They seemed to sparkle and take everything in, desperate not to miss a single moment.

Peter let himself read the message one last time. His cheeks felt moist and his lips curved upward in a rare approximation of a smile. It was the first time Stew had ever written back.

Detour

The flat landscape of Oklahoma rolled by, punctuated by the occasional tree or billboard. As the freeway slid past, Leroy took quick glances from his driving to look at the woman in the passenger seat. Susan sat staring out her window, glaring with the petulance of a small child not getting what they wanted. She had been that way since they had come out the wrong side of Fort Worth and it had become obvious that they weren't going straight back to Arizona. Now, not far from the Kansas border, her mood had done nothing but deteriorate.

Leroy had tried to start a few conversations when Susan had first gone stone faced, but had long since given up. He wasn't a talkative man, and it seemed little worth the effort just to get one word answers. The radio played quietly in the background. Slow sad country songs about losing your woman and fast paced country songs about getting drunk. Not much in between. The cab of the old pickup was cleaned as best it could be, but nothing could hide the sun weakened plastic of the dash and the permanent scuffs of long use.

The woman Leroy could see out of the corner of his eye was older and thicker than the pictures she had sent. Her hair had a bleached look to it and there were prominent crow's feet around her eyes and loose skin at the corners of her mouth. Leroy didn't mind. Such things were to be expected. He hadn't let his expectations get too high. Besides, it had been the words in her letters, not the face in her photos, that had convinced him to make the thousand mile drive from Safford to Livingston.

Leroy knew he wasn't much of a catch himself. Not many women wanted a wind burnt old cowhand who rarely got into town and spent most of his time on the back of a horse up on Mount Graham. At least the photos he had sent had been fairly up to date. Though in fairness, most were of the landscapes around his home rather than his own hangdog features. Leroy knew he was no Tennyson either. His letters had all been fairly straight forward and lacked the flowery wit that he believed most women found endearing. The landscapes had seemed like his most sellable feature. Perhaps some women were looking for a man with unexciting qualities. Leroy didn't know, he really didn't understand women, and had never bothered giving much thought to the subject.

It was lonely up on the mountain. Especially when the work was done. He had the cows and a string of good horses, but none of them could be called good conversationalists. Leroy had gone after the problem the same as he would have if he had found a broken pipe or a hole in a fence. Find the right tools, and fix it. No fuss and no muss. The ad he had put in the personals section of the *Ruralite* had been straight forward.

Lonely Arizona cowhand, age 40, seeks woman.
Quiet and easygoing, seeking the same.
Beautiful place to live.

It had been surprising the number of responses he had gotten. There were a lot more lonely women out there than Leroy had expected. But after a few letters back and forth most had dropped off, except for Susan. Her letters had been long and wordy, always at least three pages, impressive given her small handwriting. Leroy's letters had been short, though he tried to always make sure he filled up at least one page. Letters had moved on to phone calls. Leroy had done his best to hide the fact that he was about as interesting as morning oatmeal. He had told her all his favorite cowboy jokes, even the one about the dead mouse in the chili. She had seemed to enjoy them.

The "Welcome to Kansas" sign rolled past, changing the state but not the landscape. The pickup cab continued to be filled with sullen silence. Leroy watched the world roll by and ignored it. If she was going to be sullen, she was going to be sullen. A little side trip seemed like a silly thing to get upset about. There was nothing he could think of to say, so he didn't see the need to bother. Trucks and cars whizzed past on the left. The old pickup was going as fast as it could, which wasn't that impressive. Besides, if he pushed it too much, air would howl through the loose windshield seal and they wouldn't be able to hear the radio.

A blue sign whipped past on the side of the road. Susan's voice entered his ear, flat sounding, but loud in the silence. "Can you stop up ahead? I have to use the bathroom."

"Sure, no problem."

Leroy pulled the old pickup off at the freeway exit and parked it next to the roadside restroom. Susan got out, the old seat springs creaking underneath her, and slammed the door. Maybe she was angry, though Leroy couldn't figure why. Maybe not though, the old pickup's doors had to be slammed to get them to close proper.

Leroy got out too, and stood next to the pickup admiring the waxed finish on the dulled and chipped paint. He walked around his vehicle and checked the tightness of the ropes which held the blue tarp over Susan's belongings in the back. Susan hadn't come with a lot of stuff. Leroy thought of that as a positive. The three pieces of furniture that she would not part with were a squat bookcase, an old sitting chair, and a giant dresser with a vast top like an aircraft carrier. The chair and bookcase would easily fit in the living room, but Leroy doubted there was room in the bedroom for the dresser. He would probably have to throw his out, which was too bad, he had owned it since he was a boy.

All the ropes were as tight as they could be, so Leroy got back into the pickup and sat down to wait. He reached into his shirt pocket and pulled out a folded up piece of high quality magazine paper. The cattlemen's magazine always used high quality paper. He unfolded the advertisement and sat looking at it.

For Sale $500
Purebred border collies trained by Gus Stewart
Both sire and dam High Plains Cowdog Competition Champions
Concordia, Kansas

Susan got back in the pickup and slammed the door behind her to get it closed. She glanced over to see what Leroy was reading and gave a derisive snort.

"I can't believe we're making a seven hundred mile detour just for a god damn dog."

Leroy folded back up the advertisement and put it back in his shirt pocket. He ran a hand through his thinning hair, started the pickup, put it in gear, and lurched out of the rest area. His eyes remain locked on the windshield in front of him.

"Who says the dog was the detour?"

Contagion

Five jeeps and two trucks, all painted dark green, pulled into the small village on the border with Guinea at six in the evening. The doors of the trucks were painted with a red cross on a white background. The jeeps were unmarked. Men piled out carrying machine guns and split into groups of two to search from house to house. Old conical round ones and newer rectangular ones. The invaders were non-descript men. Wearing the same assortment of t-shirts, jeans, and shorts as the majority of the villagers. However, the invaders were still easily distinguishable, they wore no bright colors and all had a red handkerchief somewhere on their body. Tied around their head, arm, or leg. None of the invaders had any visible hair. Their heads and faces were shaved clean, including their eyebrows. The witnesses would later claim that there were as many as a hundred. In truth there were only forty-three.

A short average looking man got on top of the hood of one of the trucks as the invaders scurried about their business. He wore bermuda shorts and a button down shirt left open, revealing a body starting to go to fat. His face was lined and worn. A pistol hung from a belt around his waist. The witnesses would all describe him as a giant. There was no doubt who was the leader of the group. As the lappa women, in their two piece dresses, ran to their homes to protect their meager belongings, the leader's voice boomed across the village.

"We are the Saviors of Liberia. We have come to cleanse your village of the blight of ebola. We are here to stop the spread of the virus and save the people of Liberia. Those who stand aside will not be harmed."

"Ebola! Ebola!"

The shout could be heard across the village, emanating from a house of wood and sheet metal. A woman's voice, thick with emotion, yelled back unintelligibly. The crack of a gunshot echoed across the village clearing. The woman's voice changed into screaming. Another gunshot, and then silence. Two invaders pulled a jerry can of gas from the back of one of the trucks and jogged towards the commotion. The leader did not break the rhythm of his speech.

"Households that contain Ebola will have the sick ones shot. Those that have provided direct care to the sick will be shot. Their homes will be burned to ensure that it does not spread. The disease kills ninety percent of all who catch it. They are already dead. Leaving them alive just gives the disease more time to spread. We do this because we must. I am sorry that this must be done. We do not wish to do this. We cannot stand by and do nothing. We have taken the weight of this task upon our shoulders. If we do nothing, then all of us will die. Every man, woman, and child will die. Bleeding from their eyes and asses. The sacrifice of the few will save the many."

"Ebola! Ebola!"

More shouts broke out from houses. More shots. The leader climbed down to the ground as the first dwelling began to burn. A commotion broke out near one of the houses. Two invaders stood just out of range of a frenzied gray haired old man guarding the doorway of his house, swinging a machete wildly. The invader's voices rang out again and again.

"Ebola! Ebola!"

Another pair of invaders ran over to provide their comrades help. The gray hair's face was covered with tears and he frantically tried to shout down their accusations.

"No! No! Not ebola! Just sick! Not ebola!"

The scene lasted only thirty seconds more, then one of the newcomers raised his machine gun and silenced the gray hair with a single shot. Two stepped over the body and crowded into the doorway of the conical house. The sound of another shot and the invaders emerged. There was no laughter. No jokes or jibes. The invaders' faces were set in stone. The newcomers moved off towards the next house, and the two remaining shouted to be heard by the men waiting by the trucks.

"This one! Burn this one!"

Two invaders carrying a jerry can of gas between them hastened to obey. The old man was the odd man out. The majority of the villagers just stood and watched in silence. Theirs had been one of the villages that had fled to Guinea during the overthrow of Charles Taylor. They remembered how best to survive. A significant portion of their number looked more relieved than frightened.

The leader stood calmly and watched the work of his men. His face showed no emotion. A frail looking man, a lieutenant of some type by the way he held himself, with less deference compared to the others, approached.

"Titus? Titus?"

"What is it Mr. Tubman?"

"It's Jerome and Uriel. They say they cannot do it. They say they cannot cleanse a house."

The leader gestured for Mr. Tubman to show him the way. The two men jogged to a house of mud with a roof of dried palms. The wooden door was open, but the two invaders in question stood outside, their guns pointed at the ground, staring off towards the trees and undergrowth at the edge of the village clearing. The leader cleared his throat, and for a moment the two men met his steely gaze, but then stared down at their feet with shame. The leader's voice was low in volume, but carried across the village for all to hear.

"What is going on? Why do you not cleanse this house?"

The two men looked at each other, and then back down at the ground. The leader waited for a few seconds, and then cleared his throat again. The bigger of the two, the one they called Uriel, with shoulders like a bull and arms the size of his comrade's legs, licked his lips, nervously played with the safety on his machine gun, and raised his gaze to the level of his leader's bare chest.

"Our apologies sir. Neither of us can do it. They are children sir. They look like my son and daughter."

Uriel started to cry. The leader looked from the sobbing man to the quiet skinny one by his side.

"Is this the same for you Jerome?"

Jerome kept staring at his feet, but nodded his head in affirmation.

"They've been shunned sir. Their mother is dead inside and it's obvious that no one else has been providing any care. I'm sorry. I just can't do it. When I went in they looked at me with their eyes full of fear and hope. One is already half dead, and the other two aren't far behind. I just can't do it."

Jerome began to cry as well. The leader pulled his pistol out of its holster and chambered a round with a resounding click. He turned and walked into the darkness of the doorway. Mr. Tubman and the two crying men waited outside. Three quick gunshots, and the leader re-emerged into the waning evening sunlight. His face was frozen in a mask of calm, only flawed by the twitching of one eye which went still after a few seconds. He put his pistol back in its holster and drew the two sobbing men into a hug so their heads rested on either side of his.

"It is okay. It is okay my friends. Tomorrow you will burn instead of shooting. I know that this is hard. It is okay."

The three men stood holding each other for nearly a minute, and then the leader broke away and walked back towards the trucks and jeeps. Mr. Tubman followed, his shrill voice rushing out ahead.

"This one! Burn this one!"

The leader leaned against the side of the forward most jeep and let his gaze sweep across the village. Twelve burning buildings belched black smoke up into the sky. The rolling dark billows seemed to form into the faces of laughing devils until they rose high enough to be scattered by the wind. The invaders had been in the village for less than fifteen minutes when they finished their task and began to move back to the jeeps and trucks. The villagers continued to watch in silence, most standing and staring, a few sitting near the fires, crying or staring blankly into the flames. The leader lifted back up his bullhorn and shouted to be heard above the crackling of the burning buildings.

"This village has been cleansed. If anymore become sick, kill them immediately and burn their bodies and homes. You are not committing murder. They are already dead. We are doing what we must to save our people. To save our nation. To save our world. Any supplies that you can give us will be welcomed. If any of you want to join us to help, then come."

Some villagers rushed back to their houses and brought back bags of rice and other food. They handed them to the invaders in the jeeps and trucks. Others stood in unmoving knots and watched, their faces betraying nothing. Two men walked forward with bags of meager belongings slung over their shoulders. The invaders helped them into the back of one of the trucks. The leader's eyes gazed one last time across the village then gave the signal. The jeeps and trucks roared to life and left the village behind.

The convoy moved slowly up the road from the village. The road was in poor condition, treacherous even during the day. Three jeeps were in front, followed by the two trucks, followed by the remaining two jeeps in the rear. The men sat quietly as the convoy moved. As quiet as devout men sitting in church. They gripped their machine guns tightly and eyed the darkening forest around them. The leader sat in the front passenger seat of the second jeep in line, his back rigid, watching fireflies catch light as nightfall fell across them. Mr. Tubman sat just behind him, studying a large map unfolded on his lap with a flashlight. Twenty red x's clustered in one corner. A deft movement of Mr. Tubman's hand added a twenty-first to their number. Mr. Tubman kept his voice low so as not to break the quiet.

"Tomorrow will be different. Tomorrow will be a larger town. About five thousand people. Zor..."

"I do not want to know the name of the town Mr. Tubman."

"Yes sir. There is a hospital there. Many of the surrounding villages are bringing their sick."

The leader nodded, but said nothing more. Mr. Tubman watched him as he gazed out at the fireflies with the wonderment of a child. The leader held out a hand and kept it perfectly still. A firefly landed, sat and rested for a while, and then rejoined his brethren in the air. The leader smiled fondly.

After a few hours the leader called a halt. The sounds of the motors were silenced and the men clambered out to set up camp. The wood was wet so it took some time to get the fires lit. A watch was set and the men set to work making their dinner of rice with palm butter and sweet potatoes. A banana bunch was pulled out of one of the trucks and the yellow fruit were broken off and passed around.

The leader and Mr. Tubman sat by themselves next to their own small fire. Food was brought to them, but otherwise they

remained undisturbed. They talked quietly to each
other, planning the next day's strategy and discussing tactics.
The men would be told the plan in the morning. The men sat
about their fires and talked quietly amongst themselves. They
sat spaced widely apart, doing their best to avoid touching each
other. There were no sounds of laughter or other signs of
happiness. The mood of the camp was somber and introspective.
The new recruits, illuminated only by the flickering flames, had
their heads and faces shaved. An old man, one of the oldest
members of the group, explained the duties they were to
perform.

"You will help burn the buildings and defend the convoy and
our leader. The most important thing to remember is not to
touch the bodies. Do not touch the bodies and avoid touching
their belongings. Ebola is spread by touching the fluids of the
body."

The smaller of the two recruits was full of questions, he was
at most sixteen years old. The silence of the camp made him
uneasy.

"Will I get a gun?"

"Yes, we will provide you a weapon. It will be your duty to
keep it in good working condition. We will show you how."

"Will I have to shoot anyone?"

"Not at first. You will not be part of the shooting teams until
the time is deemed right."

"Who will decide?"

"Our leader."

"I'm not sure I can do it. I don't know if I can shoot
someone."

"We all do it. We all have taken on this responsibility and
we all do our part. This is the decision of our leader. He knows
that by doing so we all share the load, and it is lighter than it
otherwise would be. This is the law of the group. If you cannot,
then you must leave."

The other new recruit was a man in his mid-thirties. He stared at the dancing light of the fire and listened. He had his own questions, especially one that he wondered about the most.

"But where does the leader come from? Why does he do this thing?"

"Nobody knows."

The big man named Uriel looked up from the pot of rice that he was cooking. His eyes flashed in the darkness.

"I heard that he was once an officer in the military. A hero from the civil war who fought to overthrow Charles Taylor, but never committed any atrocities. He was sent here to establish order and help fight the ebola. But as things got worse, he saw what had to be done. He resigned his commission and cleansed his first village with just five men."

The skinny man named Jerome leaned forward until his features were visible in the firelight. He waved his hands dismissively.

"No, no. Our leader was no soldier. He was a doctor from Monrovia. Trained at the university. He was sent here by the government to help treat the disease, but people kept dying and finally he was forced to accept the truth of the situation. He killed all the patients at the clinic in Voinjama and started gathering men."

A third man chimed in from across the fire.

"I heard that he came from a village near the border with Sierra Leone. When people in his village started getting sick he told his friends and family to trust the doctors that came to treat them, but then his wife and daughter died. It is said that he saw the truth then, and that the first village that he cleansed was his own."

A fourth voice came from an unseen speaker at the next fire over.

"He was sent by god from heaven to save us all. He is the tool of the almighty."

The old man shook his head.

"It does not matter where he came from. All that matters is that he is here now. All that matters is that he is going to save us all. Nothing else matters."

The men whispered back and forth and finished their meals. One by one they drifted off to sleep, waking only to switch the watch. The fires slowly died, leaving just the light of the fireflies, and were nothing but ash by morning.

The men woke with the first light and consumed the cold remains of the evening meal, scraping the pots empty before cleaning them with sand and water. The morning chores finished, they lined up to be checked. Mr. Tubman, wearing rubber gloves, worked his way down the line, feeling foreheads. If a member of the group felt too hot, he took their temperature using one of several thermometers that he boiled every night. The morning check done, the leader stepped forward to give the men their orders for the day. The leader went through the instructions three times, handing out assignments and making sure each man knew what he was supposed to do. Mr. Tubman stood to the side and slightly behind the leader, holding his lanky frame in a loose approximation of a military stance of attention. As the leader spoke it began to rain and soon everyone was soaked. Once the leader was confident that every man knew his job, they loaded up into the jeeps and trucks and headed down the muddy road.

The going was slow. The precipitation had turned the dirt roads into bogs. The men rode with reticent anxiety. Muscles taut with tension that increased as they moved closer to their target. Tropical forest fell away and the convoy entered the town. The dirt streets were mostly empty, most people were staying dry out of the rain. The few that were out and about quickly ducked inside the nearest building or around the nearest corner when the convoy rolled by, hiding from the heavily armed stern faced men, remembering the horrors of a world a decade in the past. The vehicles splashed through growing puddles and threw mud behind spinning tires.

The convoy entered the hospital grounds and the invaders piled out, forming a perimeter. Haggard looking nurses and technicians watched from windows and doorways in mute horror and curiosity. They had heard tales from the forest. Stories about the slaughter told by the mobile clinic and villagers bringing in their sick from the countryside. They were tired. Months of battling the virus without rest had left them only ghosts of their former selves. Bloody death after bloody death. Unending application of disinfectants. A lack of needed resources. The failure to give proper care to those not infected by ebola. Only half of their original number were left, the rest dead or disappeared, slipping away to save themselves. The nurses and technicians knew that they should feel something about the armed men at their hospital, but emotions were a luxury that had been surrendered long before.

The hospital was made up of fourteen buildings. It had been destroyed during the civil war, but since rebuilt with donations to assuage the guilt of those lucky enough to be born in countries filled with wealth. Rain drops pinged off zinc roofs. Walls of gray concrete and white stucco shone brightly against a background of greens and browns, showing only the beginnings of the unstoppable jungle rot. Grounds that were once well cared for showed signs of neglect and decay. Untrimmed bushes, scattered garbage, and tracks of mud leading across stairways and verandas into every doorway.

The leader casually walked with six of his men to the administration building, moving with the confidence of a man who knew where he was going. His eyes did not bother to read the large letters next to the door that declared Lutheran Hospital. He paused in the dryness of the veranda to wring the water from his clothes and wipe his feet on the mat, before walking through the doorway into the white tile interior of the waiting room. The waiting room was nearly empty, vacant benches along three walls. A fat nurse sat behind her desk, listening to a radio which emitted the jazzy horns and multiple guitars of highlife music. She stared at the leader and his men as they walked in and approached her desk, unflinching and showing more signs of annoyance than fear. The leader stopped in the center of the room and stared down at her authoritatively.

"Administrator?"

The fat nurse nodded and exited the waiting room through a door that she pulled shut behind her. After a few minutes she returned with a man of Liberian descent wearing a blue dress shirt and khaki slacks. By the way he held himself it was obvious that the man was kwi, civilized, a member of the upper crust of Monrovia. He undoubtedly spoke good English, was at least nominally Christian, and used only cash for all his trades. He was a tall man. He gazed down at the leader from high above, and noted the machine guns held by the four nervous men with an air of disinterest. The leader and the kwi stood and stared at each other for close to a minute. Finally the leader grew bored of the game and broke the silence.

"You are the administrator?"

"Yes, I am the administrator of this hospital."

"I was under the impression that the administrator was from India."

"He died."

"I see."

The men stared at each other, mute again. The fat nurse sat back down at her desk and went back to listening to her radio, ignoring the proceedings around her. The kwi waited patiently and casually checked his fingernails for dirt and grime. The leader seethed inwardly at the arrogance of the kwi, but did his best to retain an air of calm to match that of his tormentor.

"Do you know why I am here?"

"Yes."

"Then you will show me to where you have quarantined the ones with ebola?"

"No. I'm afraid I cannot do that. This is a hospital. They are our patients."

"They are already dead. Keeping them from me will not change that."

"Perhaps. But that is not for me to decide. In the meantime, it is the duty of my staff and I to do all we can to save them."

"Your staff will not be harmed. I know they are trained in the proper quarantine methods."

"That does not matter."

"You are a stupid man. If you do not show me I will just be forced to kill every patient at this hospital. Is that what you want me to do?"

"You do whatever you think you must do, but I will not help you in any way."

The leader nodded in understanding, and then pulled out his pistol, cocked it, and shot the kwi in the head. Crimson sprayed across the white wall behind him and the body fell to the floor. Blood started to flow across the dirty tile. The leader put his pistol back into its holster and turned towards the fat nurse who was staring at the place the kwi had been standing.

"You will tell me where those with ebola are?"

The fat nurse looked at the body on the floor and then up at the leader's angry gaze. She nodded, got up, and motioned for the men to follow. She led them across the grounds to a long building near the middle of the hospital compound, pointed to a large tent against the short end, and walked away. The leader watched her go, and then led his men into the tent. Inside were portable showers, countless bottles of disinfectant, buckets and brushes, and the door into the building.

The building was a long single room with forty beds on either side. Living corpses inhabited all but three, IV's running from hanging bags to needles in their arms. Some seemed alert and in good health, others lay on the edge of death. Four figures stood amongst the beds dressed in yellow plastic suits, white rubber gloves, floor length aprons, rubber boots, hoods that covered their entire heads, and goggles covering their eyes. One stepped forward, his white skin standing out beneath his goggles.

"Hey you can't be in here, this area is qua....."

The white man noticed the machine guns and fell silent. The leader motioned with his hands.

"If you leave now you will not be hurt. We are here to cleanse this hospital."

The four figures walked quickly out the far door. Many of the more alert patients raised themselves up, watching with growing amounts of concern. Their eyes were wide in their faces. Their breathing ragged. Several of them started hacking and coughing uncontrollably. The leader nodded and his men raised their machine guns and opened fire. Several of the patients tried to get out of bed and run, but were quickly cut down. Others lay still, too weak to do anything but watch. Once all the runners were down the men started working their way up the line of beds, shooting those too weak to move with a single shot to each head. The leader watched from the doorway in silence.

Near the far end one of the men gave out a cry of surprise and dropped his machine gun to the ground. He dropped onto the bed and pulled a small woman into his arms. She hung limply like a rag doll as he cried and clutched her to his chest, repeating her name between his sobs.

"Anna. Anna. God no. Anna."

The leader rushed forward, yelling as he ran.

"Lionel you idiot. What are you doing? Have you gone mad?"

Lionel looked up, blood from the woman's nose smeared across his cheek.

"My sister. She's my sister."

The leader stared at the quivering form and the sick woman. His face showed no emotion. He pulled out his pistol and cocked it. Lionel's eyes filled with fear and panic.

"No sir. Please. She's my sister. My sister."

The crack of the bullet echoed across the room. The body of the sick woman fell back into the bed without a face. Lionel started to scream, but the sound was cut short by a second gunshot. Lionel fell on top of the body of his sister. The leader turned without a word and marched for the doorway, motioning for his men to follow. It was no longer raining when they emerged from the tent. The leader motioned at a knot of men waiting with the jerry cans.

"Burn it."

The men rushed forward to obey and the leader walked back across the grounds to the administration building. It was empty except for the body of the kwi. The leader sat on a bench next to the wall and stared down at the dead body. The radio on the fat nurse's desk buzzed with the rapid fire words of the DJ and the manic forward rush of the music. The leader sat and saw nothing, feeling the backed up tears push forward against ducts long since closed off. The music died and was replaced by the ever calm tones of the BBC news at the top of the hour. Mr. Tubman walked in the door and rushed over.

"There you are sir. I've been looking for you. We need to burn the other buildings. Should I have the......"

The leader did not look up, but stared at the spray of blood on the far wall. The leader's voice was quiet. Barely louder than the radio.

"Shut up."

"Sir?"

"I said shut up."

"We discussed this. If we don't burn the hospital then the villagers will continue to bring their sick here. The more they move the more likely they will be to infect others. The hospital must be.…..”

"I said shut up Mr. Tubman. Tell the men we are leaving."

"But sir…"

"Now."

Mr. Tubman turned and walked out of the administration building. The leader could hear Mr. Tubman's shrill voice screaming out commands. The leader stared at the spray of blood on the wall intently, as though it was a piece of modern art that he was trying to understand. He pulled out his pistol and held it on his lap, wondering what the cold metal would feel like in his mouth. The radio news anchor continued talking, a background buzz that seemed to grow and fill the world.

"…….doctors report at least 7,000 known cases at this time spread across Guinea, Sierra Leone, and Liberia, as well as several new cases reported in Nigeria. The head of the World Health Organization stated at a recent press conference that this is by far the worst outbreak of ebola in history and that the situation remains dire. Experts are predicting……"

The leader got up, holstered his pistol, turned the radio off, and walked out the door into the sunshine.

Three Contacts

I lay in bed with the taste of stale booze on my breath and the smell of second hand cigar smoke in my hair. I'm awake, but not yet ready to admit it. It's a Saturday morning, so it does not matter. I don't have to move forward with the day until the afternoon. My clothes sit in a heap upon the floor. My pockets short by thirty dollars, lost in last night's monthly poker game. The pile waiting for the wash has mixed with the pile of those waiting to be folded and put away, and it is becoming more difficult to discern between the two. There is a pressure in my bladder, but I refuse to give into its siren call. I refuse to abandon my refuge of warmth and comfort.

The talk had strayed, as it always does at such things, to questions of monogamy and love. Sorting feelings and impulses concerning marriage, intimacy, and children into some kind of recognizable mass that can be used to propel us all into the confusion of the unknown. I add only quips to the conversation. My opinion subconsciously downgraded due to my status. Of the seven men at the table, I am the only one that is alone.

Should we do it or should we not? Should I take a leap or retreat back from the edge? The world has saved me from such questions, and there is a part of me that is grateful.

My bladder can no longer be ignored. I rise up into the coldness of the air and plod on stiffened joints to relieve myself of the most immediate of life's pressures. The toilet flushes, I break off four squares of toilet paper, and return my body to its refuge. I do what I need to do. Solve the loneliness of the body, knowing it will do nothing to solve the loneliness of my mind. The hands of an array of former lovers brush lightly across my skin, their heads kicked back in ecstasy until the moment that I cover the toilet paper with a million possible futures, all cut off and made impossible by a short flash of endorphins that soon fizzle out like soap bubbles floating through the air.

The former lovers do not leave, but march in an array before my eyes, each bringing with them a host of memories both good and bad. What makes me so different than the other six? Has it been lack of luck, lack of the ability, or just a curse for past transgressions? I don't know. They all march past. The one who was hot and cold, the one always on the edge, the anxiety ridden one which I had loved, and the one who gave me comfort. The one who had never meant anything to me at all, the one who ran away, and the one to which I could never explain why the one before ran away. All the ones that were just to meet my bodily needs, the crazy one that broke into my house, the one who I cheated on, and the one who made me better, but from whom I still walked away.

Each has been fully reviewed, categorized, and analyzed. Patterns noted. Habits observed. Trying to understand. Trying to see where it all began. At what junctures did the world split in two? At what moments did I take the wrong path down? They cluster around me and grab me as they can. Some eyes filled with hate. Others filled with sadness. They hang from me like an anchor, their voices low, nearly a whisper in the wind. Alone.

Alone. You will always be alone. Look at all the wrong you've done, and look at what has happened even when you do what is right. There is no escape. This is your fate. I scream and try to fight, but their grips just become tighter. Dragging me down further into the depths of questions with no answers.

I rise up from my bed and go to start my day. A busy mind is a distracted mind. A distracted mind is one that can continue moving forward. I flush the million lost futures down the toilet, and shower away the dirt and grime jamming all my pores. I stand in front of the bathroom mirror, open the medicine cabinet, and take out the case that holds my eyes. First I open the one marked *Left*. I always start with the left. My finger reaches in, breaking the membrane of saline solution, and pull the contact out.

Two contacts sit in my hand. I stare down at them in puzzlement. Two contacts in the one marked *Left*. The wheels of my mind start turning and I chuckle at the inebriation of my past self who put both contacts in a single side of their container. My eyes are slightly different. It will just be a simple solution of trying each one in each eye, and seeing how clearly I view the world. Just a single test is needed to turn my hypothesis into theory. I open the side marked *Right*. A single contact stares up at me. I pull it out and lay it next to the other two on my hand. What the fuck?

It makes no goddamn sense. I have two eyes, but three contacts. Solutions run through my mind. They are monthly contacts, it is only the third of the month, maybe one of the old ones got caught in the case when I threw them away. Maybe contacts are made of layers, and those layers separated. I'm using a different kind of solution than I normally use. Maybe my house is haunted, and the ghosts have tired of smaller pranks and decided to up the ante in their own little ghostly show.

I turn my hand and drop the contacts into the garbage, pull a new set from the cupboard, place them on my eyes, and don't give the matter another thought. Wondering about it won't solve the mystery, and I have shit that I need to do.

Mea Culpa

The remnants of a home cooked meal sits in the garbage where they were scraped from two plates now sitting in the sink, waiting to be washed and made clean. The uneven cadence of the rain beats against the windows as the storm outside slowly gains strength. It was predicted that it would be a stormy night, all the signs pointed towards bad weather. The man and the woman sit on the couch, holding wine glasses and chit chatting. A half empty wine bottle sits between them.

> *Dear Lauren,*
> *I saw you a few weeks ago sitting in a bar. You were enjoying a drink and chatting with some friends. I thought about coming over and talking to you. But it has been so long. I chickened out and said nothing.*

They talk about their work and their weekly foibles. The woman laughs and tucks a strand of hair behind her ear. Her smile is coy and her eyes are devilish. The man drinks deeply and refills his glass, hiding the tremors in his hand. The man makes conversation, but he does not hear all of the replies. Inside his head a single thought is swimming. It surfaces insistently and tries to find its way out, but the way is blocked. It is something that must be said. It is something that must be pushed to the front. Instead he tells another joke.

> *Seeing you for the first time in a year brought*
> *back a lot of memories. It got me thinking about a*
> *lot of things. Things that I should have done a*
> *long time ago.*

"I need to talk to you about something."
She leans herself forward to better hear.
"Yeah, what is it?"
 Her eyes go from blissful to a mixture of confusion and expectant interest. The first words have tumbled out of his mouth and he is trying to force out the rest. He has to go forward. The opening move has been made. There is no going back.
"I just wanted to talk about us." Her eyes grow wary and the smile on her face becomes a straight line.
"I've had a lot of fun hanging out with you and getting to know you over the past two months."
"I've enjoyed it too."
"But I feel like I need to tell you that where this is now, is probably as far as it's going to go."

> *I'm sorry for the way I told you I didn't want to*
> *pursue a relationship with you anymore. The way*
> *I handled the situation was hurtful, immature, and*
> *in no way respectful to you or your feelings.*

"What exactly do you mean by that?"

"I mean what I said. Personally I don't want to pursue this relationship past what we are currently doing."

The pair sit in silence and the man finishes his wine and pours more from the bottle. She stares at him, and then turns her head and stares at the knick-knacks on the mantle. The silence makes him uncomfortable. He can hear the gears grinding in her head. A sudden shift without the use of a clutch. It is as though her brain has seized up. Complete and utter quiet. The only sound the pushed air of both their breathing and the heating vents.

"Are you okay?"

"I don't really know what I'm supposed to say."

I knew that I had gone about it in a fucked up way immediately afterward, but I was too chicken shit to do the decent thing and apologize. For that I apologize as well. I hope you can believe me when I say that this was a case of personal stupidity, and not malice.

The silence goes on. He stares at her, and she continues to stare at the bric a brac on the mantle. A wooden buddha, a jade dragon, a fan from Korea with a painted picture of two men watching a group of women bathe in the river, a wooden man in a barrel with a spring loaded penis, an alligator head, a little statue of Saint Patrick, a fossil with a fish on it, and a little wooden statue of four monkeys in a row. One holds his hands over his ears, one his mouth, one his eyes, and one his genitals. Hear no evil, speak no evil, see no evil, do no evil.

"Where did you get that fan?

This is not how he expected this to go. Accepting words, crying, yelling, screaming, laughing, all of these could be expected. A hundred scenarios had run through his head throughout the day. Her yelling and insulting him, her crying and him trying to provide what comfort he could, her laughing and saying that she felt the same way. Small talk was not part of the list of expectations.

"It was a gift from a group of Korean businessmen who visited my office here a couple of years ago."

She takes a drink from her wine glass and sets it back on the table. "What about that little statue of the bishop?"

"You mean Saint Patrick?"

"Is that who it is?"

"Yeah."

"Why is it up there?"

"I went to Ireland a couple of years back. I bought it at a tourist stand at the foot of Croagh Patrick, the tallest mountain in Ireland. It's about twenty five hundred feet high. I started climbing up, thinking I'd only go up to a little rise. But I just kept going until I reached the top. It was the middle of winter, so I was up in the fog and everything was covered in snow. There was a little church up there. I'm not that religious, but something felt special about making it to the top. I had that little statue in my pocket. I blessed it in the snow."

She turns her gaze and looks at him. Her lips bend into a smile. The smile makes him even more uncomfortable. He doesn't know what to think. Nothing is going like he imagined it. He doesn't know what to do.

> *This is something that I have felt bad about for a long time. What I should have done was tell you that you are an amazing person who was very enjoyable to be around, but that I felt the way each of us wanted to live our lives was very different and that dating just wasn't working out for me.*

He puts his wine glass on the table next to hers. Anxiety courses through his body. He does not know how to react. He does not know what to say. Panic is setting in. She is just sitting there, looking at him, the woman he just told he wanted to break up with. The woman he had stupidly invited to his house for a home cooked meal already knowing that he planned to end it. Why had he done that? What had compelled him to make such an offer in the dwindling heat of post coital bliss the night before? What is he supposed to feel? What is he supposed to do?

The brain hits critical and overheats. Emergency shutdown. Automatic protocols take over. He leans forward and suddenly they are kissing. Lips embraced and hands moving furtively against each other's bodies. Flashes of consciousness. They are off the couch and she is leaned up against the wall, one leg kicked up against his side. They are in the bedroom and her shirt and bra fall to the floor. He guides her to lay back on the bed and he follows her downward. No words. No thoughts. Just a primal need to make the world make sense.

"Wait a minute." She breaks their embrace and they stare at each other in the light from the hallway. "What did you mean by what you said earlier?"

"I meant what I said. That what we're doing now is as far as things are going to go."

He can see the gears break free and the wheels of her mind spinning once again. Her face contorts from one of pleasure to one of anger. She stands up and towers over him. She seems like a giant. It was a bad move. It was the wrong decision. He wishes he could squeeze himself down until he disappeared.

"So what the fuck do you think you're doing?"

"I don't know."

*I should have as well talked more openly about
how my thoughts and feelings regarding the*

relationship were forming as they did, rather than keeping my mouth shut and releasing them like a fucked up surprise party.

She puts back on her bra and she puts back on her shirt. She walks out to the living room and sits down to put back on her boots. He follows her out into the light, bare chested.

"How long have you known this?"

"Awhile."

"Jesus Christ. We're you just leading me on for sex?"

"No."

"Why the fuck did you make me dinner tonight?"

"I don't know."

She puts on her coat and wraps her scarf around her neck. She fumbles with the door. It always sticks. It's always hard to open. He moves forward to help her but with a violent motion she gets it herself. She looks back as she walks out of the door.

"You need to get your fucking head examined and learn how to better communicate."

The door slams and he stands there and listens to the sound of her car door opening and closing. The sound of her car starting and driving away. He goes and sits on the couch. Her umbrella sits on the coffee table where she left it. He looks at it and lets the storm of emotions roll over him. He shakes uncontrollably for several minutes. Once the storm passes, he picks up the wine glasses and carries them to the sink.

It showed a total disregard for your feelings.
Again, I am very sorry.

Old

The hospital room is stark and bare, few ornaments or accessories beyond what is needed. The walls are an inoffensive cream color which does little to hide the buildup of dirt, scuffs, and chips which shows how long it has been since they were last painted. The bed is the newest thing in the room, a monstrosity of modern medical science covered in hard plastic with rounded edges. A collection of cards and flowers sit on a metal end table under a sagging half inflated mylar balloon emblazoned with "Get Well Soon." A few machines on wheels stand in one corner and a metal bar runs along the ceiling with the faded hung curtains pulled back.

"Is that where you do your pull-ups," the younger brother jokes?

The older brother smiles and the old woman glances up from her chair at the two standing tall men long enough to give a half hearted curve of the lips before looking back at the old western playing on the television. There are other chairs farther in, but neither of the two tall men venture any further than just inside the doorway. The parties sit in uncomfortable silence, both brothers trying to think of something to say and failing in not falling victim to the draw of the moving images on the screen hung high up on the wall.

"I wish they'd let me turn off this television. I've never been one to watch a lot of television," states the old lady before returning her attention to the stated hated box.

Both men stood awkwardly quiet, unsure what to say. The stunted wrinkled woman before them with the frizzed out hair the color of steel is not the woman they remember when they think of their childhood days. She is not the woman in her seventies who still climbed the fruit trees to cover them with nets to save their bounty from the birds. She is not the woman in her eighties who still rode her horse up in the hills, chasing out the cattle from the canyons and the rills. The old lady in the chair is but a shadow, a memory of what has been.

The older brother is the first to take a venturing leap forward, breaking the silence like breaking bread. "We thought we'd just come up and see how you're doing. How have you been?"

The old woman looks up distractedly as though her mind is slightly out of focus and she's unsure how to feel about the visiting situation. "I've been fine. They've been taking good care of me here and I've been looking forward to getting home to my cat."

"That's good."

"That's good."

Both brothers' voices sound together, same words just slightly off each other's beat. The room goes back to silence except for the voices from the hanging box.

When one is young falls are simple things, a quick brush off and then get up again. When one is old this is no longer true. A fall can take you from independence to sitting in a chair with a sensor hooked to your shirt so they know when you get up to use

214

the bathroom. One fall can lead to another, a downward cascade to the darkness of beyond.

"I'm sure you will be home soon. We've heard you've been giving them hell."

The brothers smile once again and the old lady gives another ghostly smile as well. They're mother had told the story to them just that morning. The story of how the old lady had started taking off her shirt to use the bathroom, so the nurses wouldn't know she was doing it and rush in to give unwanted help. Another pause, another silence, another shifting from foot to foot.

The younger brother looks up at the television, but feels guilty so looks away. He doesn't know what to say so his eyes rove the room looking for distractions and possible sources of inspiration. Out the window a tree stands bare, its leaves stripped off by the season. Its branches like grim skeletal hands scratching at the window with each puff of breeze, looking for a way in. Past the tree the view is of the city below the hill where the building sits.

"At least you have a nice view."

"Yep."

The woman below is not what she once was. She has always been stunted and wrinkled, but she never used to seem so old. It's the little clues that show the difference. The hair no longer permed or dyed black. Once their father had walked in on her while she was dying it, she always did such things on her own, and she had offered to dye his as well if he would like. Their father had chosen to keep his own salt and pepper hair. It wasn't just the looks, it was the vibe that she threw, the aura that surrounded her which her love of life imbued. Where once it had been so strong, now it seems deflated like the leaky mylar balloon.

The old woman breaks the silence, undoubtedly wanting to be polite. The two nice young men had come to visit her and old habits learned in childhood from long dead parents living only in her memories must still be kept. "You know, this isn't where I want to be. I'd really rather be home and working. But I guess you have to do the best with what you have. There's just some things you cannot change. So I guess I'll do the best that I can."

The two men stand in silence for a bit, neither sure what to say. Finally the older brother replies with a simple, "I guess so."

"I wish I had the controller to this television. It would be nice to turn it off."

"Are they taking good care of you?"

"Oh yes, they keep me well fed and check up on me all the time. Probably for the best because I keep forgetting things. I guess it's all part of getting older."

"Is there anything we can do for you?"

"No, they're taking pretty good care of me. They keep me well fed and there's a nice library of books down the hall. They bring around a cart so you can choose one if you want."

The back and forth seems to have tired out the old lady and she looks back up at the television. The men glance at each other, then at her, and then at each other again before letting their eyes follow hers to the flickering light. It's a strange and uncomfortable feeling that permeates the room. Both men wonder how long they need to struggle with the difficult situation. They both feel guilty at such thoughts, but both cannot help but feel like strangers in the presence of someone who was like a grandmother to them. There is a feeling that the old lady is wondering the same as them. How long do they have to stay?

"You two sure are tall," says a croaking voice from behind them in the hall. The two men turn and an elderly lady sits hunched over in a wheelchair, half melted like an icecream cone left out in the sun.

"Yes, we've been told that before," replies the older brother.

"They gave us ham and potatoes today for lunch. Rodney does the cooking and he does an alright job though the potatoes were a little lumpy. I prefer my potatoes without lumps in them."

"That sounds very nice."

The two brothers turn back to the old lady in the chair, the one they came to visit, guiltily ignoring the smacking of lips behind them and the creak as the wheelchair moves further down the hall. The younger brother looks at the older brother then back to the television. The younger brother doesn't like these places. These halls of healing full of husks of death. He'd rather be most anywhere else, but duty and memories hold him in place.

The old lady breaks away from the hanging box once again, feeling like it's her turn to move the stilted conversation forward. "So what do you two gentlemen do?"

Even when you know to expect something, it never prepares you for actually seeing it in person. When the men were children the husband of the old lady had his mind begin to unwind. Alzheimer's their mother had called it when she tried to explain to them why a man they had known their entire life suddenly didn't know who they were. The old lady kept him at home the entire time as he slowly forgot all that he was. Finally one day he died, but long after he was no longer truly there.

"I work on the ranch with Dad," replies the older brother.

"I'm an economist in the city," says the younger brother.

"Well, that sounds nice," states the old lady, and then back to the television once again. "I wish I could turn off this television."

It's become too much for the younger brother. Too much reality for one day. The need to leave has overcome his guilt for wanting to be somewhere else. He looks at the older brother and the older brother looks at him. The older brother's eyes finally nod agreeance.

The younger brother's voice sounds strained even in his own head. "Well, it was good seeing you."

"Take care of yourself," adds the older brother.

The old lady looks at them again and smiles. For a moment it seems that for her the entire world comes back into focus. The age melts away and everything is as it once was. "You know I'm awfully proud of you boys. You've all done so well for yourselves."

The men say their thank yous and goodbyes are exchanged. The younger brother is loath to leave though just moments before it was what he desperately wanted. They walk down the hall and the old lady goes back to her television. Out the big glass doors and into the car in the parking lot. Keys into the ignition, but the younger brother doesn't start the engine.

The older brother speaks. "You know, I think she was just saying all that about the television because she didn't want us to think all she's doing is sitting around and watching it." The younger brother nods and tears roll down his cheeks. The older brother looks at him. "You alright?"

The younger brother nods again. "Yeah, I'm alright. Just a lot to take in."

"I know."

The younger brother starts the car and they head off down the hill. Both the men are silent, alone in their own thoughts. The younger one is not alright, but there's nothing he can say. He cannot say the things that are in his head. He knows that he never wants to be in that position. He knows he never wants to sit in the lobby waiting to get in, his failing body like a prison and his keen mind slipping and going astray. He knows that no matter how long you last the end is always the same. Fear and confusion while one waits for their lives to be reclaimed. Looking at it in the face, he knows that old age is not for him.

Fantasy

The man who will never be walks past the woman who never was on the street. They both pause and look back. Part of both wants to turn and keep going, but the pause has been too long. Old pain and aged hurts bubble from the depths. Subconscious hands move unconsciously across old scars that are unseen by the wandering eye. They stand and stare. Neither sure what to say. He is the first to find his voice.

"Hi."

"Hello."

Their voices are quiet. Tentative. Neither sure what to say. What to do. The primitive part of the brain screams to fight or run. To raise one's voice or simply turn and walk away. Both the woman and the man do neither. He can see the fear in the woman's eyes, windows the color of the ocean. He knows that the look is mirrored in his own. He will have to make the first move. It is as it has always been.

"How have you been?"

"I've been fine." A quiet pause. He begins to feel awkward as she stares down at the ground. "How about you?"

"I've been pretty good."

"Well, that's good."

"Yep."

Silence once again. People move by on either side, but none dare break the bubble between the two. Neither seem to know what to say. All the things that he's always wanted to say surge up in him, but crest before they reach his mouth, and fall back unsaid. There is no point. There is no reason. Just old pains, and aged hurts. Better to let them go. Better to continue the slow process of burying them down deep where they can no longer be felt. He raises one hand and starts to turn away.

"Well, I guess goodbye then."

"Goodbye." Her voice is as quiet as a whisper. His rotation makes her disappear out of sight as though she had never been, and he begins to take the first step away. Her voice comes again, louder this time. "I'm sorry you know."

He turns back and looks at her. He is unsure what to say.

"It's okay."

"No, it's not. I didn't treat you well, and I never once said I was sorry. All you did was care, and I treated you like shit."

"Thank you. That actually means a lot to me."

Silence once again.

"Thank you for trying."

"I'm glad I did."

The two ghosts stare at each other across the few feet of concrete. The years wash away and it all comes flooding back. The good and the bad. The happy and the sad. A wave of emotion and regret too long held below the depths. This is the time. This is the time to say the right thing. He can feel tears in his eyes, and can see tears in hers as well. He tries to smile, but it only goes halfway.

"Well, I have to get going. It was nice to see you."

"Yeah, it was nice to see you too."
"Goodbye."
"Bye."

The Accident

Jesus Antonio Ruiz Fuentes lightly tapped the brakes of the old pickup as he approached the turn. The roads were icy, especially on the corners shaded by the rolling hills. It had taken a little while to get used to driving on the icy roads. The trick was to slow down before you needed to. They didn't get a lot of ice back home. The weather was too warm. Sometimes too hot, but rarely ever too cold, at least compared to here. Jesus could remember sitting outside as a child back home, staring up at the stars and shivering. It didn't seem so cold now. Back home you never had to wear a thick coat, long underwear, and gloves. Things were different here.

Mariachi music blared over the pickup's radio. The radio didn't even have a tape deck. Jesus would have to remember to change it back to the boss's AM talk radio station before he got back. The boss didn't want to hear mariachi music when he turned the key. The boss wasn't a bad man to work for, he was usually friendly and always treated Jesus fair, he was just particular about certain things. The boss employed three Mexicans, but didn't speak any Spanish. Most of the communications were either through Jesus' cousin Javier, who spoke very good English, or via gestures and diagrams drawn in the dirt on the ground. Jesus was fairly quick. He could usually understand what he was supposed to do.

It had been warm when Jesus first arrived. The summer was hot, just like back home. A dry heat similar to being inside an oven. Everything had seemed more familiar when he had first arrived. Javier had sent him a letter, telling how much better things were up north. He had promised Jesus a job if he could only make it up. Jesus had left home without a second thought. There was really no reason to stay. Javier had been right. This place was different, but it was better. His first paycheck had seemed like a princely sum.

The pickup rolled out of the hills down onto the big flat that stretched to the big river far away. The highway and power lines stretched ahead of him in a straight line, empty fields on either side. When he had first arrived the fields had been full of hay and alfalfa. Now they were barren, yellow, and covered with frost. Wheel lines sat inert in the fields, waiting for the change of seasons to spring back to life and provide the water needed to turn the yellow back to green. Far ahead a bank of gray fog hugged the ground, a cloud too weary to traipse across the sky.

Just ahead Jesus could see the large electronic sign that overhung the road. Just fifteen more miles to go. He looked at the clock on the radio, 9:15 AM. If he didn't take too long loading the bags of salt he would be able to get back home by lunch time. Rosa, Javier's wife, always made the best tamales. Even the boss seemed to prefer them over his seemingly endless supply of sandwiches on white bread. As Jesus drove under the sign he saw a message in yellow letters flashing on its black surface. Jesus paid it no mind. He could not read English. It was probably just warning about the ice on the road.

*   *   *

It took fifteen minutes to walk the four blocks from Martha Anderson's house to the bus stop. Four blocks of excruciating pain from her arthritic hips, knees, and ankles. Fifteen minutes of risking a fall on a patch of ice or snow. One foot in front of the other. Hoping the grips attached to her shoes would provide enough traction. Move forward a step, push her walker slightly forward, move forward another step. From the bus stop it would be a ten minute ride on the number five bus down three stops. Off the bus and then walk across the parking lot to the liquor store.

Martha didn't get out of the house much anymore. Just once every three days to make her journey. The nurses with the hospice, sometimes the fat one and sometimes the blonde one with the mole, brought her groceries and prescriptions every Monday. They didn't bring her everything she wanted. When her kids, who all lived in other states, had hired the hospice she had asked, but they wouldn't do it. Hence the journey. It was worth the risk.

The trees along the street were all bare, their bark covered with a sheen of frost. Thin layers of snow covered the ground, with patches of wet yellowed grass emerging here and there. The exposed skin of Martha's face felt cold. Jack Frost nipping at her nose. The world beyond a block away was hidden by the fog. To her eyes the neighborhood seemed more rundown than it used to be. The once brightly colored houses seemed drab, and old couches sat on the porches, surrounded by steadily growing piles of empty Bud Light cans. The old names came to Martha's mind as she passed each house. Smith, Jones, Cranston, Rogers, and Denton. All gone. Now Rodriguez, Perez, Gonzalez, Mendoza, and Herrera. She was the last.

When she got to the liquor store she would tell the clerk that it was for Henry. The clerk would lean down and grab a fifth of cheap vodka, so cheap that it smelled like rubbing alcohol, smile, nod, and put it in a paper bag. They both knew it was a lie.

Henry had been dead for fifteen years. Martha wasn't sure why she told the lie. She wasn't sure why she felt the need to, just as she wasn't sure why she hid the bottle in the upper tank of the toilet when she got home. It just seemed easier that way. Less fuss. She could medicate in peace, and for a little while not feel the weight of the changing world around her.

A young Mexican man sat in the middle of the bench at the bus stop. He wore baggy pants and an oversized shirt and coat. His skin was dark and a wispy black mustache covered his upper lip. Martha tried to hide her discomfort. She wondered why he wasn't at work. For a group of people stealing jobs, they seemed to do a lot of sitting around, she thought. The Mexican didn't move as she shuffled up. He sat looking at his shoes. Martha said nothing. She just stood and glared down at the inconsiderate man she considered a foreigner. The Mexican finally looked up, his mouth slightly agape. They sat looking at each other for several seconds until the Mexican scooted over so she could sit down. He moved slowly. Martha harumphed as she sat to show her displeasure that the simple gesture of respect seemed to require all of his effort.

Martha was careful to make sure that no part of her touched the man next to her on the bench. Her sinuses were clogged, but she imagined that he smelled. She checked her watch, holding her wrist far from her face and squinting so she could see the hands on the last gift Henry had ever given her. It was 9:15 AM. The bus should be arriving in the next few minutes. Martha sat and clutched her purse tightly, so the Mexican wouldn't get the idea into his head to try and steal it.

The siren started quietly, but quickly rose to a fevered pitch until it seemed to fill the air and envelope them in a world of concentrated sound. The first thought that popped into Martha's head was air raid. The noise sounded exactly like the air raid drill she had heard once while visiting Portland, back when she was young and pretty. Henry had taken her there for one last hurrah before he had to report for training to go fight overseas. She could still feel the taste of his kiss on her mouth that night, the first time they made love. That was a long time ago, over fifty years. The war was long over. This was no air raid.

The Mexican sat bolt upright at the sound of the alarm. He looked at Martha and she could see his lazy eyes were filled with fear. He knew what the siren meant just as well as she did. Dogs across the neighborhood started to howl. The Mexican looked away and then looked back at her. He chewed on his bottom lip as though deep in thought, and then jumped up and bolted down the street as fast as his legs would carry him. Martha watched him go, just one more piece of proof that the world had gone to shit. She reached up and turned off her hearing aid, muting the world around her. Martha sat on the bench at the bus stop, and calmly waited.

The table hit the back of Gary Johnson's legs as he felt himself tumble backwards onto its flat surface. His forearms caught the weight of himself, and then Katherine as she fell on top of him. Her hands were desperately roving across his body, never staying in one place long. Scrabbling as though trying to gain purchase. Her mouth was on his and her kisses were deep and desperate, as though she was trying to suck the life from him, so hard that he could feel his lips bruise from the pressure. Gary's hands sat uselessly at his side, shocked into submission, unsure what to do. Her lips moved down his neck, sucking and biting. Gary looked over her shoulder, across the white back of her blouse and the navy blue swell of her skirt. His eyes focused dumbly on the counter, where his coffee mug, with the floral design on it, sat still steaming next to the coffee maker. In the background the wail of the sirens rose and fell in their unending undulations.

Katherine. The woman who just a few minutes ago had given him a dirty look when she had caught him catching a glance as she adjusted her stockings. The woman who had told the entire office and made a joke about it when he had asked her out a few months ago. The woman who had told him flat out that she was too good for a man like him. Katherine. The woman scrambling to keep her perch on top of him on the table in the break room. The woman inundating him with her taste, scent, and feel. Gary felt as though he was drowning in her essence. Madness. It was all madness. The entire world had dropped off of its axis, spinning wildly into chaos.

The look Katherine had given him when she caught him looking at her while she adjusted her stockings had soured his stomach. She had been sitting at her desk across from his. He had glanced up just at the right time. Her skirt pulled up, the white of her upper thigh, a flash of colorful red panty. Katherine. The woman he wanted. The woman he needed. The woman he fantasized about. The look. Full of distaste and loathing. The fantasy tumbling down into the harshness of reality. Looking away. Feeling ashamed. Getting up and fleeing into the breakroom. He didn't have time. Mr. Sanders wanted the update on the Myers account by 9:30. Coffee. Coffee made a good excuse. He was just getting up for coffee. He was not fleeing. He was not running away.

Gary had just finished filling his cup when the scream of the siren overcame the background tapping of keyboards and the hum of the refrigerator. The sound had frozen Gary to the spot. He knew what it was. He knew what it meant. Run away. Escape. Get out of there. Death is coming. The reaper is on the loose. Flee. Flee as fast as you can. Gary was rooted to the spot. The siren rolled downward into quiet and then rose again into full force. He stood and stared dumbly at the sign on the fridge. All food will be thrown out each Friday. Gary's mind had stopped working. All he could think about was the bag containing his lunch in the fridge. A turkey sandwich on rye, a bag of off brand ranch flavored corn chips, and a can of Coke.

Katherine had come into the break room after the third cycle
of the siren. Her eyes had been filled with fear. Her body
shrinking into itself. Desperate to hide. She had stood in the
doorway and they had stared at each other as the siren rose and
fell in the background. Gary had wanted to yell at her to run, to
get the hell away, but his voice would no longer work. The fear
in Katherine's eyes had been replaced by a sudden flash of
madness. It had seemed as though her body suddenly doubled in
size. She had swollen up as the life she was soon to lose
suddenly fought loose of its bounds. Gary had had just enough
time to put his coffee cup down before she had thrown herself at
him.

Madness. This was all madness. They needed to
run. Needed to escape. They were going to die here. Katherine
finally managed to gain purchase on the table. Her knees pulled
themselves up on either side of him, straddling his body. Her
beautiful form reared up before him and her hands gripped tight
and ripped open his blue cotton dress shirt. White plastic
buttons flew through the air. She reached down and pulled her
blouse up over her head, revealing the tan lace of her bra
underneath. Gary reveled in the sight and felt shame at the pale
pudginess of his own body. A minivan next to a Ferrari.

Insanity. This was all insanity. They had to escape. Gary
tried to force the words from his mouth, but then her lips were
on his again, their tongues tangling so no words could come. It
was too late. They couldn't escape. They couldn't get
out. There was nothing he could do. He was trapped. He
wanted to leave, but could imagine nowhere better to go. He
was stuck in a fantasy where the driver was fear, not love. Fear
of the end. Fear of the emptiness to come. Desperation to fill
oneself with as much life as possible before the world came
tumbling down. Gary felt his hands rise on their own accord.
He felt them encircle her waist and draw her further in. He felt
her hands desperately working at his belt. His mind screamed

for him to run, though he knew he couldn't outrun what was coming. There was nothing he could do. Nothing but let the madness take him.

"Fuck you Julia."

Mr. Garner's face was red and his eyes were full of spite and anger. The statement had come out with the hard suddenness of a slap upon Mrs. Nelson's psyche. The words were a yell in everything but volume. Mr. Garner was angry, but he had not lost control. No one outside the tight circle of teachers had heard the outburst, the quiet words lost in the ambient noise of nervous teenagers and the plaintive scream of the siren.

Mrs. Nelson let her eyes glide around the circle of educators beneath the basketball hoop, looking for support. All seemed tense and on-edge. A few looked her in the eye, their faces neutral, but the majority looked away, finding their shoes more interesting than the ongoing drama. Even Mr. Cavanaugh, the gym teacher, always her ally in the past, looked away, pretending to notice something else that required his immediate attention. He turned from the circle and stalked off towards the students arrayed on the gymnasium bleachers.

Mr. Garner stood staring at her, waiting. Mrs. Nelson took a few deep breaths to calm her nerves. She needed to stay calm and collected. Mr. Garner was a bully. He had always been a bully. Someone had to stand up to him. Someone had to keep their head. It should have been Principal Myers, not her, but Principal Myers was sobbing out of sight beneath the bleachers, cracked from the moment the sirens began. Mrs. Nelson wanted to panic too. How could any of them not want to? How could anyone keep it together knowing what was going on outside?

"For the last time Pete, you know the rules." Mrs. Nelson kept her voice low, quiet enough that no one outside the circle could hear her words. "No one goes out once they come in. The doors get locked after five minutes. We all went through the training. We all know what we are supposed to do."

"For Christ sakes Julia. There's still six students out there. Don't you give a damn. We've been through roll call twice and they're still fucking out there. You know what's going to happen to them if they stay out there. Do you really want that on your conscience?"

Mrs. Nelson stifled the need to reach out and slap Mr. Garner as hard as she could. It wasn't a fair thing to say to her. This wasn't the position she wanted to be in. Did Mr. Garner think she was stupid? Did he think she didn't know that her words were dooming those six unlucky kids. She wasn't supposed to have to make these calls. It wasn't her job. Her job was to educate. Mrs. Nelson wanted nothing more than to curl up under the bleachers next to Principal Myers and cry, but she couldn't. Someone had to take charge, and no one else was stepping up.

"We aren't risking everybody for six slackers who probably cut class to go smoke cigarettes out by the dumpsters."

Mrs. Nelson regretted saying it as soon as it came out of her mouth. She could feel many of the other teachers start to really look at her, their shoes forgotten. She could feel what little support she had waver. Mr. Garner, sensing the opening, struck with precision.

"Is that what this is about? Would you be acting differently if these were some of your star kids? Is it because these kids don't meet your standards?"

It was true, the six students missing didn't exactly have the best reputations. Truants who cared more about getting high off glue than bettering themselves in any way. But that wasn't the reason she was condemning them to die. The words of the U.S. Army lecturer that had come to the school last year filled her mind. Ten milliliters, that was all it took. His description had been very graphic. First it would just be just a runny nose and a feeling of tightness in the chest. This would be followed by nausea and difficulty in breathing. The victim would lose control of their bodily functions. Defecation, vomiting, and seizures. The victim's body would cease to function, and they would die of asphyxiation.

Mrs. Nelson turned her head and looked back at the High School's student body, minus six, arrayed on the bleachers. She could see them all writhing and choking, dying in minutes. She wondered how many of them knew? How many of them understood? Surely most of the brighter ones, the ones that paid attention. Surely they had to know. How long until the shock wore off? How long until everything descended into chaos? Most likely not one would ever see their parents again.

The sirens were enough to drive one mad. They were all on the edge. Someone had to keep their head. Someone had to be the anchor. She would never see her husband again. In her mind she could see him. Convulsing on the side of the road in his orange vest. His hard hat flung into the ditch. The rest of the county road crew all flopping around him like dying fish. Mrs. Nelson forced the thought from her head. She couldn't think about it. She had to keep her sanity. She turned to face Mr. Garner again.

"You know the rules Mr. Garner. We're not risking thirteen hundred kids for six."

"For god sakes Julia. This entire room is under positive air pressure. If we open a door air goes out, not in. We're not putting anyone at risk."

"The U.S. Army installed the pumps, and the U.S. Army told us to lock the doors after five minutes." Mrs. Nelson stood as tall as her small frame would allow. She put her hands on her hips like she was lecturing a disobedient student. "Who do you think knows better? You or them?"

"We can't leave them out there to die. I'm pretty sure I know where they are."

"The rules say we lock the doors after five minutes. It is time to lock the doors."

"Fuck you."

This time the statement wasn't controlled. This time it echoed through the gymnasium, bouncing with frustration from the rafters. The entire student body became silent and all eyes focused on the two teachers facing off. Mr. Garner turned and ran across the basketball court. His footsteps sounding loudly through the silence. Mrs. Nelson made no move to stop him. Mr. Garner ran to one of the doors, one of the four doors that sat in each corner of the gymnasium, and opened it. The sound of air pushing itself past him into the hallway beyond could be heard by everyone. He gave one last look back and then disappeared through the doorway. The door swung closed behind him and the sound of whooshing air stopped.

Mrs. Nelson looked at the circle of teachers again. They all stood staring at the door. She looked up at the thirteen hundred students, minus six, huddled in their great mass, unsure what to do. Mrs. Nelson walked purposefully across the basketball court. The click of each footstep ricocheting loudly in the silence. As she crossed center court she looked down at the painted picture of a pitbull inside a purple circle lined with yellow.

Mrs. Nelson arrived at the door Mr. Garner had left by, and without hesitation, reached out and locked it with a resounding click as the bolt drove home. Nobody moved. With every eye upon her, looking nowhere but straight ahead, she walked around the gymnasium, and locked the other three doors as well.

Lucia Falto Perez clutched her crying daughter closer to her chest and repeated the well worn lines of the Hail Mary again under her breath. The words had been repeated so many times in the last seven minutes that they had lost all meaning except for the small bit of comfort their familiarity afforded her. The words did nothing for the baby in her arms. Too young to understand the words, too young to know what was happening, but still cognizant that something was wrong. The words did nothing for her husband Luis either, who was releasing a steady stream of Spanish curses into the air as he worked frantically with the duct tape and plastic.

Lucia held her hands over little Silvia's ears, hoping to block out the words of her husband and the constant wailing rise and fall of the siren. Silvia just cried louder and pounded her tiny six month old arms against Lucia's chest. Lucia's cheeks were wet with tears and her front was soaked with sweat where she held her baby close. She wished she could collapse too. Fall to the floor and curl into a tiny little ball, crying and screaming, but she couldn't. All she could do was sit on the floor and rock her baby. Lucia's heart was beating out of control and her breath was quick and erratic. Her head felt light, and with every word of her silent repeated prayer she felt more and more like she was going to faint.

Luis pulled the plastic sheet he had just finished cutting tight against the window frame and cursed violently. He had measured it wrong. It was a little too short. Lucia said nothing. It wasn't Luis's fault. It should have been cut to the correct dimensions years ago, but it wasn't. Whoever had lived in the apartment at the time of its delivery had put the white cardboard box, stenciled with CSEPP Emergency Kit, unopened in the coat closet on a high shelf. Maybe the two of them should have done it when they moved in last year, but they hadn't. It was always something to do another day. An exercise in futility that no one ever thought they would need. Now it was all they had.

Luis tried to stretch the plastic and cursed again as the duct tape attaching it to the other side of the window broke away. He brushed his hand across the frame, resticking the tape to it. It was cold in the apartment, but droplets of sweat flowed from his black hair across the skin of his face and neck. Lucia watched

Luis's quick clever hands pull more tape from the large silver roll and add it to the growing layers. Tape holding on plastic and tape holding on tape. He added more to the other side, securing the plastic and closing the gap between the edge and the window frame with a bridge of tape. With the window covered he started applying the duct tape around the door as quickly as he could.

They had lost several minutes in finding the kit. Lucia had been in the bathroom, getting ready to take Silvia to her mother's so she could go to work. Luis had been in the bedroom, sleeping, resting before he had to start his swing shift at the potato plant. He had moved quickly when the alarm had gone off. Lucia had frozen, staring at herself in the bathroom mirror, mascara applied to only one eye. Her first instinct had been to run and grab Silvia. Luis, in just his boxers and a t-shirt, had started tearing apart closets, looking desperately for the box they had found when they had first moved in.

The emergency kit didn't contain much. Sheets of plastic, an exact-o knife, a roll of duct tape, a set of instructions in Spanish and English, an emergency radio, and five cotton masks which Luis had snorted at derisively and thrown across the room. The emergency radio didn't work. The batteries were dead. Lucia had tried to change them as her husband measured the plastic by eye and started cutting it frantically, but it took C size and all they had in the junk drawer was AA. Another oversight. Another mistake. It was too late now.

Luis was never still. With the front window and door done he grabbed the plastic, knife, and tape, and ran into the bedroom to cover that window as well. Thankfully the apartment was small. Lucia had never been glad of that before. It had always seemed so tiny and crowded. Lucia could hear Luis cursing from the bedroom, a steady percussive rhythm to the bass beat of the siren and the high pitched wail of Silvia.

Lucia stared through her tears at the window covered in plastic. It was obviously a rushed job. The plastic was slack in the middle and the tape was creased and hanging loose in several areas. Lucia had trouble imagining it keeping out a fly, let alone a monster they couldn't even see. Lucia knew that she should get up and help her husband, but she couldn't. All she could do was sit, hold her baby, and cry.

In her mind she could see the monster floating with the breeze. The steel gray clouds and wisps of morning fog became poison. The monster tapped on the window and started shaking the doorknob, wanting in. For the briefest of moments a thought flashed through her mind. She saw herself getting up and filling the tub with warm and soothing water. She saw herself looking at the rippling surface, doing what had to be done, saving Silvia from the suffering that would soon be floating through the windows and door.

She banished the thought from her mind and started shaking, horrified that it had existed at all. Hope. She must have hope. Things were going to be alright. Lucia tried to start the Hail Mary again, but could not get herself to picture the words. The horrible thought came again, blocking out everything else. Lucia began to scream, holding tightly to the bundle of warmth in her arms. Their cries joined into one and drowned out the world around them.

Ned Cox sat in his easy chair, listened to the siren and smirking to himself. He had been right. Everyone else had been wrong. His dumbass coworkers, his half-wit brother, the idiots on their video poker machines at the Cozy Corner, they had all laughed and called him a crazy fool. Who was the crazy fool now? Who was the idiot? Not the guy with the basement filled with canned food and jugs of water. Not the guy who had read everything he could get his hands on about what exactly it was the government was storing out at their depot just outside of town. Not the guy sitting pretty in the chemical warfare suit, that was for damn sure.

Ned felt another rivulet of sweat trickle down his back. The suit was rubber and plastic. It was built to keep him safe, not for personal comfort. Sarin, VX, mustard gas, none could do him any harm as long as he stayed in his suit. It was military grade, bought off ebay from some schmuck in Baltimore. Ned's nit-wit brother had laughed when he had seen it. For his brother, when the government said they were safe, it meant they were safe. Ned knew better. The guys handling Agent Orange back in Vietnam had been told they were safe. The guys that went to Iraq, now suffering from Gulf War Syndrome, had been told not to worry. It was all just a bunch of bullshit. Just new crap piled on top of the old crap.

The house was dark. All the shades were drawn and both the front door and back door were locked. Ned's hand rested on the shotgun in his lap. A Beretta RS-200. A military model. The weight in his lap made him more comfortable. He hoped he wouldn't have to use it. Ned wasn't even sure if he could get the thick rubber fingers of the suit's gloves through the trigger guard. It was better to have and never need than to need and never have. That was one thing his time in the military had taught him. Always be prepared, and don't waste time worrying about the fools that aren't.

It was too bad about some of the fools. Gary Pepperidge for example. Gary was a good drinking buddy down at the Cozy Corner. Like Ned, he'd been in Vietnam, and like Ned he had a healthy dose of cynicism. Gary had gotten involved in the class action lawsuit when news of the construction of the incinerator had gone public. Plans to destroy the weapons of mass destruction like they were just common garbage. Gary had wanted him to get involved too, but Ned had not wanted anything to do with it. He knew well before the strike of the judge's final gavel how everything was going to go down. He hadn't felt like wasting time or money on such frivolities. Gary was an idiot, but at least he wasn't just another sheep.

When the siren had gone off it had taken Ned less than three minutes to put on the suit. He had been practicing since it had arrived in the mail last year. It wasn't hard when you knew what you were doing. All it took was repetition. Training the body until everything was habit instead of thought. He had then stomped out into the living room and sat down in his chair, the sweat already pooling around his feet.

The blinds had been open when he had first sat down. Ned had watched his neighbor, some younger guy he didn't know who worked the night shift somewhere, frantically trying to tape plastic over the inside of his windows. It wouldn't do any good. The emergency kits were nothing but a feel good measure sent out by the Army to keep people quiet. He had sat and watched the neighbor until the neighbor looked up and noticed him. They had stared at each other for half a minute. The neighbor hyperventilating and Ned breathing calmly. Their houses had become two separate ships, soon to be sailing in an ocean of death. The neighbor's eyes had been filled with desperation. Ned was on the ship that wasn't going to sink. There was nothing Ned could do about it. He couldn't go back in time and fix other peoples' piss poor decisions.

The look had worried Ned. Desperate people did crazy things. It had been then that he had gotten up and closed the window blinds, hiding his island of safety from the outside world, and then tromped through the darkness to his bedroom to get his already loaded shotgun.

The flash of the big red light in the corner of the control room was setting Colonel Avery Zukowski's teeth on edge. Every strobe sent a wave of pain that added to an already powerful headache. His teeth clenched so hard that he wondered which would shatter first, his molars or his jaw. The sound of sirens above ground could just barely be heard through the layers of dirt and steel overhead. He had ordered the alarm in the control room silenced soon after it began, but he could not turn off the flashing red light. His right thigh ached from where he had plunged in twin shots of atropine and pralidoxime. The shots had been wasted, he and the three men in the control room were safe from anything going on above. It didn't matter, regulations required them to inject themselves as soon as the alarm went off.

"Mr. Hou, what's the time since initial?"

At the sound of his name the back of the black haired man, sitting facing away from the Colonel at the leftmost seat of the control console, visibly stiffened. Coming to attention even as he remained hunched over his display.

"Just hitting ten minutes sir."

The Colonel's attention shifted to the brown haired man in the center chair.

"Mr. Gerhing, what's the readings from the tanks?"

"HD, GB, and VX all still showing green sir."

"What about the sensors?"

"All sensors still show clear."

"Then why are these damn alarms still going off?"

"Not sure sir."

The answer annoyed the Colonel. He had not expected an answer. He was just thinking out loud. The Colonel did not admonish the younger man. There was a time and a place for everything. All of them were already on edge. This was supposed to be a cakewalk assignment. An easy tour of duty. Most of the men considered it boring. Sitting on their asses in the middle of nowhere. Disposal wasn't even supposed to start for another four years. It sure as hell wasn't boring now. The Colonel could feel the tension in the room. Only their training was holding everything together.

Part of the Colonel wanted to call the all clear. The computers were showing that everything was fine. Everyone had checked in and none reported hitting the alarm. The system was designed to automatically go off if any of the sensors scattered across the depot detected anything, but the computer should have recorded which sensor had been set off. Nothing made sense. In his gut the Colonel felt like it was all just a false alarm. The computer system they were using was new. It had only been installed three months ago. There was a good chance that it was still a little buggy. But what if he was wrong?

"Mr. Hou."

"Yes sir."

"Try calling the state highway department again. We need to get in touch with those dumb bastards pronto."

"Yes sir."

The Colonel tried to settle his mind so he could think. He desperately needed something to distract himself with, time to let his subconscious sort through everything and let it all fall into place. The control room lacked any kind of distractions. It was a small room. Just big enough to hold the four men and their equipment. Bare concrete walls only covered by two large maps, one showing the Umatilla Chemical Depot, and the other showing the surrounding area with the depot at its center. A red circle fifteen miles in diameter surrounded the base. Inside the circle was thirty-five thousand people, spread across six towns and numerous scattered farm houses. How many was it when the base was first built in the forties? Fewer, that's for damn sure, but undoubtedly still some.

"Mr. Shelton."

"Sir?" The blonde man in the right hand chair turned partially in his seat, holding one hand to the large earphones on his head, looking back at his superior. The Colonel had never noticed before how green Shelton's eyes were. It seemed strange to notice such a thing at a moment like this.

"What's the latest report from the teams?"

"Team Three reports Igloo 3 clear, Team Four is still working its way through Igloo 5, Team Two is on its way to Igloo 7, Team Five is still at Igloo 21, and Team One has just started checking Igloo 13."

The Colonel's eyes darted across the map of the depot, landing on each spot as Shelton named it. In his head he could see each of the three man teams, bundled up in their rubber NBC suits, working their way through the banks of small tanks holding thirty-seven-hundred tons of chemical death. One man would be wrestling with a small cage containing a rabbit, the equivalent of the canaries the miners use to carry with them down into the depths. An organic warning system. The Colonel didn't envy the men on the surface. Even with how cold it was they'd still be sweating their asses off in the heavy layers of the chem suits. The fifteen men were the only ones moving about the base. The rest were all buttoned up tight in various bunkers. Everyone had checked in safe. Thank god for that. It would take the five teams several hours to check all the igloos. The Colonel didn't know what else he could do.

"Mr. Hou, have you gotten through to the damn state highway department yet?"

"No sir. The line is still busy."

The Colonel cursed under his breath. What kind of idiot gave access to the system to the state highway department without setting up a direct line. It had been the district's hick congressman who had come up with the idea of giving the state highway department access to the electronic signs that the Army had set up at the edge of the kill zone. The Congressman had wanted the signs to be used to warn about road conditions. Some Army PR jackass upstairs had jumped all over the proposal. The brass were desperate for anything that might put a good spin on the whole situation. The civilians weren't supposed to have access to the alarm system, just the signs, but the Colonel was running out of ideas.

"What's the time elapsed now?"

"Just over fourteen minutes sir."

The man in the center grunted and mumbled something under his breath.

"What was that Mr. Gehring?"

"Nothing sir."

"What the fuck did you say soldier?"

"Just that at this point it would be quicker to send someone into town to see whether or not everyone is dead."

It wasn't a bad idea. The man on the left stifled a moan. The man in the center turned towards him, realization and regret covering his face. The Colonel remembered that Mr. Hou lived off base with his family. A wife and two little girls if he remembered right. God damn it. This was not the time for this. He couldn't afford Mr. Hou having a breakdown.

"Both of you back to work. Mr. Gehring, keep checking those sensors for any malfunctions. Try to pinpoint what set off the alarm. Mr. Hou, keep trying the state highway department. I want..."

The man on the right's voice was loud and shrill, nearly a scream.

"Sir! Sir!"

"What is it Mr. Shelton?"

"Team Two reports their rabbit has died at Igloo 7."

The Colonel felt every muscle in his body go tense. His heart began trying to break free of his chest. He could feel his breath become short and for a moment he could imagine that the control room itself was contaminated. Mr. Hou dropped the phone and started crying. The Colonel desperately tried to shove down his panic. He desperately tried to keep his mind working.

"Steady Mr. Hou. Those damn rabbits die if you look at them the wrong way. They've got to be just as stressed out as we are."

The Colonel knew he had to regain control of the situation.

"Mr. Shelton."

"Sir?"

"Instruct Team Two to get another rabbit to double check."

"Yes sir?"

The man on the left looked up at the Colonel. His eyes were watery and big tears flowed down his cheeks.

"Sir. My family sir. My family. Will they be all right?"

The Colonel looked at his soldier. He wanted to lie. He wanted to tell him everything was going to be okay, but he couldn't. He had barely been able to choke out his claim on the rabbits' overall robustness. He just stood and stared forward, unable to meet Mr. Hou's eyes. Mr. Hou looked at the map. The Colonel could see him picking out the location of his home, well within the red circle. The black haired man began to sob.

"Oh god. Oh god no."

Louie DuChene of Louie's New and Used Cars sat in his office and looked out the big glass window at his empty showroom and his empty car lot full of rows of shiny freshly washed cars. The moment the siren had gone off at 9:15 sharp everyone had disappeared. The customers, the auto mechanics, the salesman, everyone. The only one who had stayed had been Louie and his top salesman Hansen. Hansen had poked his head in briefly when the siren had started.

"What should we do boss?"

Louie had scowled and looked up from the mess of paperwork on his desk.

"Shit if I care. Can't you see I'm busy."

Hansen had let the glass door close and gone to fidgeting by the new bright red Ford F-150 in the center of the showroom.

Louie had gone back to his paperwork. After about three minutes Hansen had disappeared too. Louie didn't hold it against him. Hansen was a family man. He had a lot more worries on his mind than the signing of endless forms supplied courtesy of the DMV, DEQ, and the Ford Motor Company.

Out in the car lot a big purple inflatable gorilla rocked in the wind against its moorings made up of yellow rope and cinder blocks. The gorilla had been one of Shelby's ideas. Not a bad one. Louie hadn't seen the point at first, but it certainly did create brand recognition. The big analog clock above the front door of the showroom read 9:26. Louie pulled open his middle desk drawer and pulled out a fifth of whiskey that was still half full. He poured himself a cap full and swallowed it down, put the bottle back, and got back to work. Louie had purchased the bottle when Shelby had kicked him out of the house. It had seemed like the type of thing somebody was supposed to do in such a situation. That had been two weeks ago.

Louie rolled his fat shoulders and felt several knots in his back pull tight. The couch in his office wasn't the most comfortable in the world, not by a long shot. It had only been for seating guests until up to a couple weeks ago. Shelby had been right about that one too. It would've been better if he had spent the extra money on a nicer couch. No matter, it wasn't really something he could do anything about right at that moment.

The dealership was quiet except for the sounds of Louie working and the sound of the siren outside. The radio had been playing throughout the lot, but the light sounds of soft rock had been replaced by a looped recording telling people to stay in their homes and to remain calm. Louie had shut it off soon after Hansen had left. Everything seemed unusually quiet. Even at night, when the lot and showroom were dark and silent, cars would still drive past on the street outside. Sometimes at odd hours. When Louie couldn't sleep he'd lay on his couch under his blankets, now tucked away behind it, and wonder where the hell anyone had to go at such an odd hour. It didn't matter. It didn't affect him and it really wasn't any of his business.

Louie made good headway on the paperwork. Without anyone coming in to bother him he got twice as much done in half the time. At 9:31 the sirens abruptly cut off. Louie thought about turning back on the radio, but decided by his continued breathing that it really wasn't necessary. Part of him felt like he should try to get a hold of Shelby. It would be a nice gesture. It might win him some brownie points. Louie picked up the receiver and his big soft fingers punched in the old familiar number. The earpiece of the phone beeped, signaling a busy line.

Louie hung up the phone and went back to work. The last of the paperwork was finished at 10:57. After the last looping signature was made Louie pulled over his roludex and started making calls, letting people know he expected them back into work that afternoon.

Man of The House

Things have reached a stalemate, though you are the only one to have reached the realization. Tiring of the yelling you storm off into the cold night, with a jacket that is too light, and the shocked silence left behind by your swift departure. Breath steaming in the chill, you climb into the family car and throw it backwards from the driveway, headlights illuminating the tan paint that was her preference. Retreating down the street before the front step can be darkened by a panicked shadow rushing forward to pull you back in. The car moves on automatic, taking lefts and rights without prior plan. It does not matter where you are going. The refuge of solitary stillness has been reached.

You switch off the radio, pre-set to her favorite station, and watch the endless rows of houses roll by, each containing lives that must be so much simpler and easier than yours. Even in the light jacket you begin to sweat, so you turn the dial down, keeping it at just enough to keep the glass from clouding up. The chill air feels good against your skin. You have always liked the cold. The constant fight of your body to maintain its

247

constant temperature. Your muscles unclench. The cogs stop turning. You let your mind free to roam.

Back to simpler times. Back to childhood days. Back to you and your brothers brushing your father's hair. The fire in the wood stove crackles, providing warmth, but sucking away the last of the moisture in the winter air. The brush is passed around. The handle plastic, made to look like wood. The bristles greasy and filled with strands of the lion's failing mane. The old man sits at the head of the dining table, back erect and eyes proud. The brush is passed into your hands. You pull some of the hair out of the brush, wait for the moment when your mother, scrubbing dishes at the kitchen sink, is not looking, and let them drop to the floor.

Each stroke lifts the salt and pepper hair higher. Lifted by the static in the air. Loud bursts of childish giggling. Your mother looks over and smiles and you even notice an upward curve on the lips of the old man. You pretend not to notice, even now knowing that it is what you are supposed to do. The insistent hands of your brother reach out, and the giggling is reduced to squabbling. The game is ended and your mother hustles her brood to the bathroom to brush their teeth. She helps the youngest at the task, but leaves you and the oldest to do it on your own. Your older brother is careful not to brush too hard, lest he knock out anymore of the loose ones like he did last week.

Teeth cleaned, you are marched back to the dining room, where the old man, his hair still frizzed and wild, reads the paper. You and your younger brother kiss your father on his cheek. You feel the roughness of his whiskers on your lips. Your older brother hangs back, unsure. The old man looks unsure as well. Your older brother leaves with just a whispered good night. Your mother tucks you in. You in the bottom bunk, your older brother in the top, and gives each of you a kiss before turning out the light. From the room of your little brother you can hear your father reading. You strain to hear, only every other word making it through the wall. Your older brother does not need stories any more, and the two of you are kept in lockstep by the sharing of the room. You feel proud that you stopped needing stories at an earlier age than him.

The car finds its way, following the curving road up onto the hill. Through the gates of the cemetery. Down the narrow gravel lane between the rows of monuments to strangers. You are far from home, and it is for none of the resting spirits that you've come. At the back fence the car stops, the headlights turn off, and the noise of the engine ceases. The lights of the city stretch outward across the flats. A tightly knit galaxy of stars, stretching towards the far horizon. You sit quiet and look out across your world.

Stand up straight. Tuck your shirt in. Keep quiet. Quit fighting. Sit still. God why couldn't we of had girls? Everyone says that girls are so much easier. Toughen up. That wasn't so bad. Quit crying. You don't want everyone to see you crying do you? Your father never cries, don't you want to be like your father?

You feel your eyes grow moist, but nothing falls. Even here they do not flow. The pumps stay off. You pound your fist on the dash. The bottom of your fist hurts, the muscles bruised. Fuck. The sharp explosion of the expletive ricochets through the car's interior. Your body tightens and shakes. You pound the dashboard once again. It hurts like hell. The blasts subside. The debris settles. The dust falls from the air. Your muscles loosen once again. You sit and look out over the city lights, trying to spot your house amongst the herd.

The old man walks into your room to yell at you to hurry up. You're going to miss the bus. He looks down and spots the old pocket knife with the cheap plastic handle sitting on the dresser. He asks if it is the same one that you were given when you were ten? It is. He tells you again to hurry up, and then leaves the room. You finish getting dressed and rush out to the dining room table to hurriedly force down a dry bowl of bag brand frosted flakes. Your father eats oatmeal, eggs, and coffee. The same meal he always eats, every day except Sundays. Your mother leans against the kitchen counter, eating toast. The air is tense. They've been fighting. They're waiting for you and your little brother to leave for the battle to renew. The arrival of the bus offers you an escape.

You spend all day in the classroom. Sitting in the middle of the room. Not up front with the overachievers. Not in the back with the slackers. You sit and stare at boobs out of the corner of your eye. You're glad you're sitting down. You get caught looking. She gives you a dirty look. You can read her thoughts through her expression. Pervert. What the fuck are you looking at? They're just boobs. Just part of the human anatomy. Not wanking material for your dirty fantasies. These are something special. These are my magic secret. I only show them to guys I like. You're not one of the guys I like. You're weird. Remember that time in sixth grade when you cried on the playground? Everyone remembers. You shift in your seat uncomfortably and try to focus on the blackboard, but all you see is boobs.

That evening is the basketball game. You're on the JV team. You spend most of the game on the bench. Your little brother spends most of the game on the court. You feel a deep sense of shame. You make sure no one notices that you feel it. You laugh and make jokes with the other benchwarmers. The coach yells at you to pay attention. The final buzzer sounds and you head down to the locker room. Your mother and your father stand in the crowd at the doorway. Your mother tells both you and your brother good job. The old man remains quiet. As you head down to the locker room you can hear your mother comment to another woman how much your little brother looks like his father. The next morning there is a small package on your dresser. It's a new pocket knife.

The windows are steaming up, so you turn back on the car. You click on the radio, and play with the dial until you find some music that you like. It's getting late. It's well past midnight. There's no reason to stay up here all night. You flip the switch for the headlights and put the car back into gear. It doesn't drive in automatic. You have to think about it every time you hit the brake or gas. Each turn of the wheel to the left and right. You feel tired. Exhausted. You're ready for bed.

Tell me how you feel. You are my rock. Why don't you ever talk about your feelings? I don't know what I would do without you. Quit trying to fix it. I hate it when you try and fix things. I'm sorry I forgot. Why don't you ever do anything for me? I just want you to listen. The shower drain is clogged, would you mind fixing it? Why don't you do what I ask? You're so selfish. Not now, I'm tired. Quit acting so weird. I'm glad that I found you. Jesus, can't you act like an adult? Act your age. I just want you to ask me about my day. Don't turn this around on me. Nothing I do is good enough for you. It's not my fault. I'm doing the best I can. I can't believe you said that. Is that what you really think?

The car pulls into the driveway. You set the radio back to her station and move the dials for the heat back to where she likes them. You turn off the car and sit for a moment, enjoying the silence. You breathe in and out a couple times, and head inside the house. She's sitting on the couch. Her eyes are puffy and red. She looks up as you come in. You sit down on the couch next to her. You apologize, then you go to bed.

Apeiron Review Interview

In the spring of 2017, a now defunct literary review published my short story *Baby*. A year and a half later, they approached me about doing an interview about the story, which they published in the spring of 2019. As often happens with such things, talking about the story was considerably longer than the story itself. Given it's about the only time I've been interviewed about a specific story, I decided to include it here.

BABY: AN INTERVIEW WITH SHAWN CAMPBELL

Back in Issue 12 of *Apeiron Review*, we featured the story "Baby" by Shawn Campbell. It's a heartbreaking piece about a family of obese individuals where a daughter pleads for permission to get gastric bypass surgery in order to help her control her weight. The mother, a frantic and overbearing woman who expresses her love by constantly feeding her children, gets hysterical every time the subject is brought up, and we see the tragedy of uncontrolled obesity play out in a display of literary fatalism.

I recently spoke with Shawn regarding "Baby."

***

First off, tell me a little about yourself, beyond what's included in your bio.

Well, I had a bit of an unusual childhood growing up on a cattle ranch, which led to a lot of facing some stark realities fairly early in life. After all, it wasn't like when my dog died my parents could just say that it had run off to live on a nicer farm. Being twenty-three miles away from the nearest gas station certainly had its disadvantages, but one of the advantages it had was that I had plenty of time to write.

What did you write back then?

A large part of my late childhood and early adolescent years were spent filling spiral notebooks with fantasy stories and *Star Wars* fan fiction that was exactly as good as you might imagine. Whatever dreams I had to become a writer I abandoned in high school to pursue pressing hormonal urges, though I did fill a journal with some angsty poems which I'm glad to say I burned soon after graduating. I did a write a little in college, but most of my time was spent somehow both getting an education and acting like a complete moron at the same time.

When did you start writing seriously?

I didn't start writing seriously until 2010, most of the early stuff being venting about a bad break up, which for some reason no literary review wanted to publish. Go figure.

No comment, but carry on.

Eventually, I shifted to writing about other things, which lo and behold, despite more rejections than I'd care to think about, started to lead to some publications in various literary reviews starting in 2013, *Apeiron Review* among them. Well, that's me in a nutshell, or at least the writing end of me. You can't give everything away in the first few paragraphs.

Now before I dive into my questions surrounding "Baby," tell me about the inspiration for this story.

The basic plot of "Baby" is derived from a story told to me by a friend concerning some people they knew, which included the O. Henry finish. When it comes to basic plot ideas, sometimes you have to sit around and wait for inspiration, and other times life just dumps something right in your lap.

I was so taken by the dark twist at the end of my friend's story, that when I got home that evening I went straight to writing, and ended up staying up pretty late to finish it. To fill in the details, I did my best to imagine what it would be like to be in such a situation, and also added in snippets from other stories I had heard from various people over the years, such as the fireman incident. Mixed all together, out came "Baby."

And what about your larger literary inspirations?

I would have to say that my overall literary inspiration is to create a feeling of sympathy for every character. I think stories should be like life. In reality there's no protagonists, antagonists, or bit players, there are just people, some of whom we get to examine closer than others.

I like a lot of uncertainty in stories, an ambiguity between the lines that creates a complex narrative. I want how a story is interpreted to say more about the reader than it does about me as the writer. I don't think a good piece of writing has to leave us satisfied. Instead, the goal should be discussion and debate, even if just within our own internal monologues. When reading, I don't think we should just be asking ourselves why we identify with certain characters. Rather, we should also be wondering why we don't identify with the rest. I firmly believe that it is an author's duty to write in ways to create the greatest opportunities for this to happen.

All right. Now the mother is perhaps the most interesting character in this story. Her twisted love feels at times like a hostage situation; she almost pushes obesity onto her children to keep them captive. She almost celebrates her daughter flunking out of college to return home.

I know plenty of people out there who have told me about their overbearing parents who are unreasonable, irrational, fear mongering, and just plain detrimental to their children. Do you feel this story is a commentary on those kind of people? What are your thoughts on the subject, what do you think and feel about what drives those kind of parents?

For my own mother's sake, I should probably say right off the bat that the mother in the story is not based on her. My mother has always been very supportive. Okay, with that out of the way, back to the question.

I agree that the mother is one of the more interesting characters, but I don't know if I agree that she basically pushes obesity on children to keep them captive. For instance, when writing the scene where Baby flunks out of college and her mother bakes a cake, I didn't see the cake as a sign of celebration, but rather the mother's attempt to show sympathy and make somebody she loves feel better the only way she knows how.

Ah, I see.

The mother was in a difficult position. She's a single parent who has struggled financially to the point where at times she couldn't even provide the most basic necessities. What kind of challenges might she have faced? How might such an experience affect someone?

When writing the mother, I pictured food in many ways to be how she showed her love. By providing all the food her children could eat, she was in affect making amends. As a single parent, the mother's food choices were undoubtedly limited by her finances and by how much time she had available. Given these constraints, she might not have been able to provide the best quality or healthiest of food, but at the very least she could always make sure there was more than enough of what she could provide. All parents want to see their children be happy, in many ways the mother was just trying her best to meet this goal with the few options she had available.

I'm fascinated by the sympathy you have for her.

This is of course not to say that the mother didn't have her problems. I think there's a strong difference between understanding somebody and condoning their actions. Baby's problem is obviously one that grew over time, and in many ways it feels like a chicken or the egg type of situation. Is Baby fat because too much of the wrong type of food was provided, or was too much of the wrong type of food provided because it was what Baby wanted?

Oh, I didn't think of that! Interesting.

Now, undoubtedly, it is the responsibility of a parent to try and teach their children good eating habits. However, at what point do we have to expect that child to start to take agency?

One of my favorite sayings is that we are not defined by what happens to us, but rather by how we deal with what happens to us. I think the central theme of the story is the question of how do we balance the necessity of being sympathetic and understanding of another's situation with our expectations

257

regarding the importance of pursuing self-improvement in the face of adversity.

The mother, as you describe her, is most certainly unreasonable and irrational. Even if we can feel sympathy for her, it does not make her actions in any way okay. However, in the end she is just a roadblock. Everyone has experience with such people or things. In the end we can't control the world around us, only how we choose to react to it.

I think overall what drives somebody like the mother in the story is a complex combination of love, selfishness, and their own unexamined issues. There's a lot to unpack with such things. On the one hand, I think the mother is genuinely scared by the possibility of Baby dying while in surgery. This is not an uncommon thing with mothers. However, on the other hand, if the mother accepts the idea that things have gotten to the point where surgery is a necessity, then she will likely have to face and question her role in Baby getting to such a point. After all, what kind of a mother would let such a thing happen?

Follow-up. Do you think the mother was just a bit of a nutcase and didn't see the harm she was causing, or do you think she might have been deliberately keeping Baby in her place to prevent her from leaving?

I think the mother was aware of her role in things, at least subconsciously, but the mind is an interesting thing when it comes to self-preservation.

Our brain wants to protect itself, and will go to amazing lengths with denials and warped perspectives in order to safeguard our views of ourselves. I think needing to see herself as a good parent is one of the major drivers in the mother's life. It's of course a natural maternal instinct, but it's kicked into overdrive by the fact that the mother feels that she failed to meet such expectations when Baby was younger.

For the mother, providing more than enough food wasn't just a matter of love, it was also proving to both herself and the world around her that she was in fact a good mother.

Ooh, another good point. I love the discussion here! So there's a bit of proving herself?

However, over the years this behavior contributed to Baby's obesity problem, leaving the mother in an increasing state of denial. It's not that she wants to see herself as a good mother, it's that at this point she needs to see herself as a good mother. Baby's want to have surgery subconsciously threatens the house of cards upon which the mother has built her feeling of self-value. Is it any wonder that her brain's response is to attack?

Let's talk food. For a story about obesity, we don't get many rich descriptions about food. I would guess that's deliberate, as the characters didn't get fat eating luxurious foods, but by consuming too much simpler foods. What are your thoughts behind that?

I don't know how much of that can of worms I want to open. I will say that my decision to not include rich descriptions of food had less to do with the quality of the food, and more to do with the assumption that people rarely get fat eating food they don't like.

Personally, there are days that I've enjoyed eating a bag of Doritos more than anything else in the world. Taste in food is such a personal thing, but I think one big factor in what we crave is what food we have available given the constraints of time and budget. Food is such a strange thing in the developed world, where never before in history has it been so plentiful or so affordable. Things like famine, or even malnutrition, are almost entirely unheard of in the United States and countries like it.

However, at the same time obesity rates have never been higher, with the worst afflicted being those on the lower end of the economic scale. There are just so many questions and thoughts to unpack with this issue that I know I can't do it the justice here that it deserves. However, in line with the theme of the story, I think a very good question is what is the correct balance between the responsibility of those who provide the food compared to the those who consume it?

A very good question. Now let me ask you a personal question.

Considering the subject matter, have you ever struggled with weight and eating? I sure have. In all honesty, this story hit home for me; I'm definitely fitter than I used to be, but at one time I did get a story published on the subject of overeating. Regardless, considering how great the obesity epidemic is in this country, as you mentioned, do you have any larger thoughts or commentary on these topics?

I've actually been quite lucky in the genetic lottery when it comes to food and weight, though like anyone, as I've gotten older changes in metabolism have forced changes in eating habits. I was also lucky in that I grew up in a household where staying active was encouraged. In this way I'm privileged when it comes to such things, something I always try to remember when thinking about them.

I think maintaining a healthy weight is like a lot of things in life, how much time and effort we put towards it shows how important to us it actually is. There is a big difference between dreaming about something and actually trying to achieve it. That being said, we all must recognize that the amount of effort that goes into achieving something is very different for each person. When it comes to maintaining a healthy weight, there are so many things involved; genetics, background, and the availability of time, just to name a few.

The amount of effort I have to put in to maintain a healthy weight is very different than somebody who has a lot more knocks against them in that department. I think it all comes down again to finding that balance between recognizing that it's a lot harder for some people to get the same results while still expecting people to take ownership of their own decisions.

I think everyone who reads this story roots for Baby's initial efforts to research the surgery, verify insurance coverage, and argue with her mother about it for so long. A lot of people share similar struggles surrounding weight loss as Baby did: genetics, environment, learned habits, etc. Yet it seems fate was just against her here. It's what makes the story tragic. What are your thoughts surrounding these almost hopeless struggles?

I think the most tragic thing for me in the story was the fact of how close Baby actually was to at least getting started on improving something she didn't like about herself. In the end, there was nothing physically or economically stopping her from getting the surgery, it was all mental.

Sure, her mother was most definitely not supportive, but at the same time, Baby was a 31-year-old woman when she died.

Beyond the emotional, there was little Baby's mother could actually do to stop Baby from getting the surgery. There are often things that get in the way of us making ourselves better off, sometimes very real things, but how often is the only thing standing in our way just our own inability to convince ourselves to try?

A great point surrounding the struggle of weight loss. Now, I want to discuss the narrator, Baby's little brother. Why tell the story through him? Granted, since Baby dies we need a way around that, but I found it interesting how he voices general helplessness regarding his mother's ways.

Even in that moment when he wants to pat Baby on the shoulder, he feels it would be pointless. It's all just so grim. Was the lens of hopelessness simply just something that made sense, or was it a deliberate choice? Tell me about that.

For me, the narrator represents all of us, the outsiders looking in. I think pretty much anybody who reads the story can agree that the brother would've been a better person if he had spoken up for Baby or at the very least shown her some support. However, I don't think it's fully fair to judge the brother too harshly for his doing nothing.

First, it is probably safe to assume that the brother has his own battles he has to fight when it comes to his mother. Second, the brother has spent his entire life in the household, watching Baby grow fatter and presumably his mother become more neurotic. How many years could any of us watch such a dynamic before we tuned it out?

Excellent point. We all eventually stop seeing things in our life.

The first break in these long-term trends is Baby bringing up the surgery after experiencing a traumatic event. However, despite bringing it up repeatedly, and even making plans for it, she does nothing, and the ending the brother has undoubtedly predicted for years comes to pass.

Who knows what might have helped Baby? Perhaps someone sticking up for her, someone offering some encouragement, or maybe even just somebody saying a kind word? However, can any of us truly say that we've never written off someone to what we believe is an inevitable end? How often do any of us want to wade into another person's problems?

By the end of the story I tried to convey a sense of the brother's regret for doing nothing to help Baby. Treating Baby's fate as unavoidable is a way for him to forgive himself. I think if we're being honest, that's something we can all relate to.

All too true. Let's end on a happy note. Tell us about any new projects you might have going on.

I've been quite busy since getting "Baby" published in the *Apeiron Review* a year and a half ago. At the time it was my tenth short story to be published, and since then I've published a further ten. I've managed to keep up on a rule of writing at least one short story a month since September of 2012, so it has been pretty exciting to see a lot of my work starting to get out there.

In addition, I recently put together a short story collection of my earliest stories, *An Unsated Thirst*, and finished my second novel, *Papaya.* The short story collection is available on my website and I'm currently shopping *Papaya* out to agents. Other than literary fiction, I've also been working on a snarky history blog called *Professor Errare* which has been up and going since early 2016.

To the *Apeiron Review,* I'd just like to take a moment to say thank you for publishing "Baby" and for taking the time to put it back out there again along with this interview, which for reasons that are entirely on me, for some reason took me longer to do than writing "Baby" itself. I look forward to at some point hopefully getting another story in your fine literary review.

As for you intrepid readers, thank you for reading, and if you would like to read more of my writing, please check out the website below.

Previously Published Works

Detour
First published in *The MacGuffin*, Fall 2016

The Trap
First published in *Bellevue Literary Review*, Fall 2016

Judgement Day
First published in *The MacGuffin*, Winter 2017

Baby
First published in *Apeiron Review*, Spring 2017

The Rodeo Monkey
First published in *New Plains Review*, Fall 2017

An Apple A Day
First published in *Cirque Journal*, Spring 2019

Man of The House
First published in *Cirque Journal*, Fall 2020

Dates Written

An Apple A Day	August 2014
The Optimist	February 2015
Apple Jacks	September 2014
Kuku Kane	October 2014
Rescued	February 2014
Drinks	October 2013
The Trap	February 2014
A Knight In Repose	January 2014
Judgement Day	February 2014
The Commodity	February 2014
Apprehension	February 2014
The Rodeo Monkey	February 2014
Return of The Snarky Scientist	December 2013
Paradise Wasted	October 2014
Arzuw	January 2014
Misidentified	January 2014
An Accident	February 2014
Transition	April 2014
The Environmentalist	July 2014
Baby	February 2015
Delayed	February 2014
Malas Noticias De Mi Amigo	June 2014
Fuck	November 2013
An Old Familiar Road	July 2013
Hank	December 2014
Everyone Is Fucking With You	October 2014
The Disease	December 2013
The Message	February 2014
Detour	December 2013
Contagion	August 2014
Three Contacts	October 2014

Also Written By The Author

The Uncanny Valley

We all know a Paul. A person who seems to see stuff that isn't there. The type the polite call quirky and the blunt call nuts. Conspiracies? He's got a few. He's got his finger on how the world really works. He knows what kind of shit is coming down the pipe. Flee across the West Texas desert to Mexico? Makes sense to him. Feel like you're being watched? You bet your ass someone is watching. Best turn off your cellphone. Troubles? Of course, that's just part of life. Doubts? No time for doubts. Shit is getting real. Get in, buckle up, crack open a beer. The only real question is, how far down the rabbit hole are you willing to follow?

An Unsated Thirst

They say that an author's first stories are their most raw. Here is a collection of S.W. Campbell's first short stories and writings. Combining both published and unpublished works, An Unsated Thirst explores victory and defeat, triumph and shame, and an unflinching view of our naked selves. How one views such stories is dependent upon the mood of the reader. Whether we are at our highs or at our lows. However, it is hard for any of us to claim that such stories are ones that we cannot identify with. Contained within these pages are parts of our lives which we try to forget, though they are an important part of what makes us whole. Such stories should be embraced, accepted within ourselves so we can better accept them with others.

Papaya

When a devastating hurricane hits the Caribbean island of Domenique, its inhabitants are forced into a singular struggle to survive and rebuild. Isolated in their midst is Ted, a Peace Corps volunteer who fled the ashes of his former life only to find himself labeled an outsider. Infatuated by the enigmatic wife of his only friend, Ted thrusts himself into a world beyond his comprehension. As obsession turns to desperation, tensions grow and Ted is forced to decide exactly how far he will go to rebuild amidst the muddy ruins.

Stumptown

There are places where people say things are better. Where the downtowns do not empty after dark and people dare to dream beyond their means. Quirky utopias where the sins of the past are washed away by gentle rains and we all go forward arm in arm together into the brightening sunshine. Distant locations flocked to by young pilgrims, unencumbered by the deeply driven roots of age, where everything will be different. Combining both published and unpublished work, Stumptown is a collection of stories about ordinary people, navigating their personal anxieties and drama in a time when uncertainties were still tucked away and not allowed to distort the sense of hope in the air. It is a soliloquy to naivete, and the belief that a better world is a place rather than an idea.

The People's Republic of 47th & Long

Perhaps the world would be a better place if we thought of ourselves less as good people, and more as lousy people who manage to do good things. My friend Leopold was always a dreamer. The pandemic and our reactions to it left us broken and divided. Most of us just wanted to feel safe again, but others dreamt of something better. Leopold was one of these. Though I think he likely joined the People's Republic of 47th and Long purely out of geographic convenience, I know once part of it, he fully shared in its egalitarian vision. All I have are his letters. Sometimes I wish I had burned them, but I didn't, so now here they are. Maybe you can find a use for them. Perhaps they can help remind you who we truly are. The good, the bad, and most importantly, the indifferent.

The Man In The Sodden Cap

The Man In The Sodden Cap is a collection of twenty-six short stories written during a period of emotional unleashing, a madcap rush to get words to the page. As with any such period of unrelenting literary expulsion, the results are a mix of emotional, personal, poignant, and inane. For many authors, these are the types of stories that often get kept in a drawer somewhere, not shared with anyone. But what use are stories if they are not shared? Individually these are good stories, but taken all together they tell the tale of heartbreak and remorse, and the need to move on. In this context, The Man In A Sodden Cap is in many ways a sequel to S.W. Campbell's first short story collection, An Unsated Thirst, a continuation and fitting conclusion to that earlier work.

More information can be found at:

www.shawnwcampbell.com

About The Author

S.W. Campbell was born in Eastern Oregon in 1983 after a harrowing drive through a fog. He currently resides in Portland, Oregon where he works as an economist and lives with a lovely house plant named Morton. He has had many short stories published in various literary reviews, some of which appear in this work, and has also self-published several books. His work can be found at www.shawnwcampbell.com.